Clara L Matéaux

Around and About Old England

Clara L Matéaux

Around and About Old England

ISBN/EAN: 9783337188375

Printed in Europe, USA, Canada, Australia, Japan

Cover: Foto ©Andreas Hilbeck / pixelio.de

More available books at **www.hansebooks.com**

IN AN ENGLISH ORCHARD.

AROUND AND ABOUT

OLD ENGLAND.

BY

CLARA L. MATÉAUX,

Author of " Home Chat," " Peeps Abroad," &c. &c.

ILLUSTRATED.

TWENTY-SECOND THOUSAND.

CASSELL & COMPANY, LIMITED:
LONDON PARIS, NEW YORK & MELBOURNE.

PREFACE.

DEAR YOUNG READERS,

I am not going to take you through a regular "History of England;" *that* you can read in as many large volumes as you like—books written by far abler hands than mine; I will only tell you as much of it as will make you more interested in the early days of old England, and help you to understand a little of the chain of events that have, in the end, made it such a civilised and powerful country.

I hope, by telling you the facts and traditions of a few of our ancient towns and celebrated castles, to enable you to attach some realities to the names of persons, famous for good or evil, which are associated with them; and I think you will enjoy seeing the pictures of places where brave and thrilling deeds have been done, where events have occurred that make them worth remembering, or that have been in any way alluded to in song or story; so that, some day, should any of you really travel "around and about," you may feel a redoubled interest in all the pleasant things you see, not merely admiring what is before you because it is a bold mass of stones, or a fine piece of scenery, but because it is part of the story of your own land. That such may be the result of your interest in this book is the earnest wish of

Your friend,

THE AUTHOR.

CONTENTS

LIST OF ILLUSTRATIONS.

RUINS OF HASTINGS CASTLE.

AROUND AND ABOUT OLD ENGLAND.

HASTINGS.

ARMS OF WILLIAM THE
CONQUEROR.

I THINK we cannot do better than begin our tour at Hastings, in Sussex, partly because many of you no doubt know it well, and partly because it has given its name to a great battle that was fought near it many hundred years ago between the Saxons and the Normans.

In earlier English history, Hastings was a place of no small importance; and we know that its navy was numerous and serviceable, even under Edward the Confessor, who made it the second of his cinque ports, the city being bound to furnish his majesty with twenty-one ships, and the services of twenty-eight men and a boy for fifteen days every year.

B

But it is later on than this that I want you to think of Hastings and its neighbourhood—in that bright September, 1066, when the venturesome Duke of Normandy sailed into the bay of Pevensey, and cast anchor hard by that ancient castle, whose foundations were then washed by the waves there, and quite unopposed, disembarked his army.

HAROLD.   *(From the Bayeux Tapestry.)*

" O'er hauberk and helm,
  As the sun's setting splendour was thrown,
From hence they looked on a realm,
  And to-morrow beheld it their own."

Can you fancy these vessels all crowded with priests and armed knights in steel helmets and coats of mail, bands of archers with bows in their hands, armourers, smiths, carpenters, pioneers, and men-at-arms — 60,000 in all ; some not over willing to follow on such a daring and dangerous expedition, yet all too proud to draw back ?

William's own ship, on which were fixed large lanterns, to make it a rallying-point for the rest, was the gift of his fair and loving wife, Queen Matilda. It was called the *Moira*, and its carved figure-head was a little boy, with a bent bow in his hand, intended to represent the duke's son, afterwards our king, William Rufus. On its sails of many colours were painted the arms of Normandy, and at its mast-head floated a banner given and blessed by the pope.

The fleet had long been delayed at St. Valery by storm and tempest, and the men had almost lost heart ; they did not feel quite sure that this expedition to possess themselves of another king's domains, to take the crown of Edward the Confessor from Harold, son of Godwin, and give it to their own lord, was very likely to be fortunate. However, the weather had cleared, and at last, after much bustle and exertion, the fleet had sailed away. The good ship *Moira*, sailing faster than the rest, outstripped the other ships, and in the morning the impatient William, coming on deck, saw no token of his friends and followers—the sea was a blank.

"Quick, captain! go to the mast-head!" cried William, to Stephen, the son of Gerard, "and tell me what thou seest."

Up went the brave skipper. "I see only sea and sky," he answered, after a long look-out.

"Wait, then!" cried the duke, "and cast anchor till they come in sight." And then he ordered spiced wine and rich food, and fumed and fretted, and tried not to seem anxious. But soon he cried once more, "Now, look out again, good Stephen, and tell me what thou seest."

NORMAN WAR-VESSEL.

"I see four vessels; and now a forest of masts and sails," was the answer.

"'Tis our fleet at last!" cried the Norman duke, joyfully; and truly, ere long, the 1,400 vessels came up, and with the royal *Moira* at their head, soon went gallantly on their way towards the coast of Sussex.

At this time William was a fine martial-looking man, about forty years of age; and as he stood there, with his heart beating high, many an eye was turned towards him, and many a bold soldier wondered as to the fortune of the mighty enterprise on which they had ventured. They were brave men enough, but very superstitious; and there was a general groan of dismay among those mailed barons when, as William was arming, his squires handed him his hauberk with the back-piece first. They thought that this accident was ominous of defeat.

"Tush!" exclaimed William, laughing their weak fears to scorn; "methinks it is rather a good omen; it betokens that the last shall be first—that the duke will be king."

As he jumped on shore his eager foot slipped, and this trifling mishap affrighted his superstitious mail-clad knights, who drew back, as they murmured, gloomily, "Dieu aide!" But Norman William, who was ever ready and artful, scrambled to his feet, and holding out the two handfuls of sand which he had clutched in falling, he cried, with ready wit, "See, sirs,

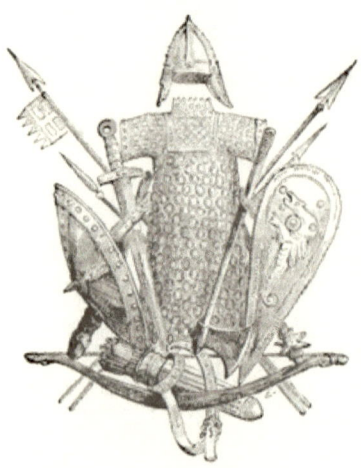

NORMAN AND SAXON ARMOUR.

I have taken some of the land; as far as it reaches it is ours!" Then they all accepted the ready omen, and pressed forward to follow their bold leader, who pitched his camp on a broad plain near, and soon erected two wooden castles which they had brought with them. One noble only began to stammer and hint of return and danger; in a moment William had struck him dead at his feet, and no one else felt inclined, or perhaps dared, to resist such an argument as that sword. Indeed, I have read that after landing, William ordered the ships forming his fleet to be burned, that his Norman followers might have no chance of return, and so must fight their best; but that, after all, may not be true.

Of course you do not wish me to describe the result of the Battle of Hastings. I am only telling you the story of the place itself.

Glance at the remains of the grand old castle perched up on that tall cliff, 400 feet high; it has been a ruin for ages. Its walls are eight feet thick. In other days many a bold knight and proud dame have held gay festival within its massive walls. History tells us that here the fair Princess Adela presided, as queen of beauty, in the first tourney ever held in England; and Stephen, the stout Count de Blois, entered the lists, and unhorsing every adversary, at last won the fair princess for his own.

But a sadder story attaches itself to this grey fortress; for it is told us that in the days of its strength and beauty, a wicked Norman lord dwelt there, who, besides many other blessings, had a fair sweet wife, whose life he made most miserable by his unjust quarrels and temper. So weary of ill-treatment did she become at last, that she entreated of the king to interfere, and order that she might be treated by her husband with more honour and respect, as became her station. But her incensed lord had his revenge; little he cared for king or wife. He, a powerful Norman baron to be defied!—he would defeat and punish them both. His heart filled with bitter feelings of revenge, and he had a great pile of faggots heaped up in the inner court, and ordered that his innocent, wronged wife and their little boy should be burned upon it in the broad daylight. His cruel orders were executed, for in those days servants were slaves, who dared not oppose their lord; but as the poor victims were burning, a high wind arose, and carried the flames across a great distance, setting the strong old castle in flames. Nothing could be done by the terrified lookers-on, for every part seemed burning at once, and the beggared lord fled the place, filled with horror and remorse, and was never heard of more. It is said that the remains of the poor lady and her child are buried in a stone coffin somewhere under the ruins.

We must not turn from this part of our coast, which the Norman William made so famous, without going some seven miles on, and visiting Battle, and the remains of the ancient abbey which the Conqueror built on the very spot where the great fight was fought that made him King of England. He dedicated it to the Holy Trinity, and to St. Martin, the patron of the warriors of Gaul. Some say it stands on the very spot where ill-fated Harold fell, as it was written on an old tablet in the parish church there :—

> "This place of war is Battle called, because in battle here,
> Quite conquered and overthrown the English nation were;
> This slaughter happened to them upon St. Celict's day,
> The year thereof (1066) this number doth array."

Battle Abbey, to which were brought seventy monks from the great convent of Marmontiers, near Tours, was endowed with all the lands for three miles round, and had many privileges ; amongst others, the abbots had the right of pardoning any criminals they might chance to meet on the way to execution. On its altar the new king himself reverently laid the sword and robe he had worn on his coronation; and here is said to have been kept " the Roll of Battle Abbey," being a list of those Norman lords, bishops, and men of high account

BATTLE ABBEY IN THE OLDEN TIME.

who accompanied William to England, which list was prepared by the monks, that they might for ever offer up prayers for those named, especially for those who died in the great battle which covered them with renown. Unfortunately, this precious roll was destroyed by fire; and of the fair abbey, which was built partly to atone for the great carnage which had taken place, and partly out of gratitude for victory, only some scattered ivy-covered ruins remain.

> " Still the proud ruins of the Abbey tell
> Where William conquered, and where Harold fell."

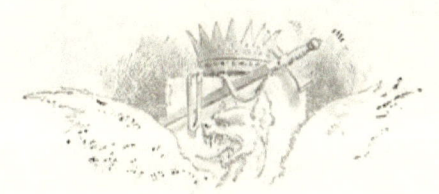

"THE WRECKER, WITH FLAME, AS OF STREAMING HAIR."

WRECKERS AND SMUGGLERS.

"Out of the black on her lee
    There flashed a glimmer of flame—
A gleam upon mist and sea,
    That flickering went and came.
And they of the ship were glad,
    And merrily tacked and bore,
With the will and strength they had,
    For the beacon on the shore.

"A perilous shore, that rose
    Sheer flint from the seething wave,
Where the sunken rocks enclose
    The bonds of a hidden grave;
And under it one crept low,
    Uplifting and waving there

A torch with its head aglow
    With flame, as of streaming hair.

"A treacherous light that glowed
    Where the demon wreckers wait:
Oh, fated vessel, that rode,
    So cheerily to its fate!
Then came a shock, and a rush
    Of waters—a cry!—and then
A crush, and a sudden hush,
    And horror of drowning men!

"Never, oh never, never!
    The winds and the rains are o'er;
The sea rolls on for ever,
    But the ship returns no more."

LET us stop at the ancient town of Winchelsea, near Hastings, and as we linger in its grass-grown streets, think of its strange history. Once it was so flourishing that it furnished ten out of the fifty-seven ships which composed the Cinque Ports navy; now it is so quiet, you might fancy the people all asleep. Long years ago, the people of Winchelsea were known and noted as wreckers and pirates. Nothing was too fierce or cruel for them. They plundered and sunk every peaceful ship that sailed by, leaving no man, woman, or child to tell the tale. And as they were so strong and desperate that no one could oppose them, they were left to work their own wicked will, and grew rich and careless, and more reckless still. But at last vengeance came for one bad deed that surpassed all that had gone before.

One bright autumn evening, in 1250, a foreign galley came peacefully sailing towards the shore; it was laden with devout pilgrims from other lands, bound to do homage at the shrine of St. Thomas à Becket, at the "martyrdom" of Canterbury, as it was called. It was a small vessel, and at the mast-head floated the banner of the Cross, and the solemn vesper hymn rose like a prayer from the crowded deck. All was peace and rejoicing as, with clasped hands, the travellers welcomed the shores of old England. But suddenly the soft notes of the hymn were changed to loud and startled cries of horror and distress, as two large and strangely-built ships, filled with fearful-looking men, bore down on the pilgrims' galley. Soon the waves were strewn with the dead and dying; the empty dismantled vessel burned low on the blood-stained waters, and the cruel pirates hastened back to Winchelsea, laden with gold and gems. The pious offerings intended for the shrine of St. Thomas were wasted in revelry and dissipation of every kind.

But hearken, children! the story goes that, as these fierce, reckless revellers sat shouting and rejoicing at their wicked feast, a sudden change came over the bright night; the moon rose red and terrible; the wild sea, changing its course, flowed twice without ebbing, making such a loud and dismal roaring and wailing on its way—sounds like the voices of murdered men seemed borne in with them—that the pirates flung aside their cups, and looked at each other, with white faces, in silent horrified amaze; while, for many miles inland, mothers drew their children closer, and wondered what strange warning was in the night wind. Then came the tempest of storm and thunder—such thunder as had never been heard in those parts before. The sky was black, yet the ocean seemed as though on fire, while the billows rose and broke like wild demon horses. Then, suddenly, above all, rose a loud wailing cry, as of the forty men, or more, who had been flung, murdered, into the depths. All

those white-faced revellers trembled at that dismal cry, that fearful roaring.
And well they might ; for, before the morning dawned, 300 houses and many
river-men were washed away by the rush of avenging waves, and people
spoke fearfully of evil Winchelsea, as of a town accursed. Again we hear
of wrong done by others of these wicked men ; for King Edward the First

THE LITTLE BOY IN THE SMUGGLERS' CAVE.

tried to awe the pirates of Winchelsea ; but, although he brought the brave
men of Fowey, and often beat and defeated them, all seemed useless, until once
more, in 1287, their foe, the wild waters, came, but this time without tempest
and warning cry, like an avenger in the night, and flowed silently over street
and quay, church and cottage, and garden, and before morning much of the
fair land, and all the pleasant green gardens that flourished on it, had disappeared for ever.

For long after this there were plenty of daring smugglers who made

COAST-GUARDSMAN.

"runs" across the sea with brandy, silks, and other things. Strange stories are told about them. I heard one about a little boy who, by some accident, wandered into one of their caverns. He did not know what all those piled-up barrels meant. But the men dared not let him go for fear of discovery; and not being blood-thirsty, as the pirates of old, did not want to kill the little fellow, so they kept him hidden away for six years. Then by some chance he found his way out, and once more reached his parents' home in safety. No wonder the smugglers were frightened and left their cave when they found that the boy had escaped, for smuggling in those days was punished by death.

But times are changed for the better. When we see the peaceful, brown-skinned coast-guardsman, in his trim dress, his big white collar, his long telescope, pacing up and down the beach, on the look-out for sails, or chatting quietly with some honest, blue-eyed sailor, it is difficult to realise these bygone days; and yet it is not so very long since this pleasant shore of Sussex was the favourite lurking-place of cruel, hardy wreckers, who often hung out death-lights to lure to destruction the homeward-bound ships, struggling bravely with the storm. The wreckers' motto was—

> "Blow, wind; run, sea;
> Ships ashore before day."

This they shouted at night, as a kind of imploring prayer; and if any poor sailor was dashed, half drowned, upon the rocks,

THE PREY OF THE WRECKERS.

no friendly hand was stretched out to save him, for it was thought that ill-luck would attend the man who saved a drowning person from the cruel waves. The smuggler was not half so cruel as the wrecker, who could look on and not help his fellow-creature flung thus helpless on the shore. There were plenty of smugglers, too, in those good old times, when honest labour was too often despised, and men risked their lives, night after night, in what they called "running" cargoes of brandy, silk, lace, and other articles, on which, by rights, heavy duties ought to have been paid to the Government. Dreadful struggles often took place among these rocks, and blood was recklessly shed by the daring, desperate men, who knew too well that they need not expect mercy, when they were in the clutches of the law.   Often,

SMUGGLERS.

too, along the coast, flared bright beacons, telling of the approach of French, Spanish, or other enemy come to attack the towns near the sea.   Sometimes the signal was merely a blazing tar-barrel or a stack of wood, set on a high place.   Only the king or the high admiral was allowed to erect these beacons, which served as signs and signals for assistance.

Here the brave Queen Philippa watched anxiously from the top of a hill, while her husband Edward won a great sea fight over the Spanish fleet laden with good Flemish cloth.   He had his two sons on the ship with him ; one the famous Black Prince, the other little John of Gaunt—not that he was strong enough to bend a bow, " but that the king loved him."   Many a brave Spaniard fell, for not one would yield to the hated Englishman, and six-and-twenty of their ships were taken.   Then, too, in 1359, 8,000 Frenchmen landed here and fired the town, slaughtering so many of the people, that the lane down which the corpses were carried to the graves is still known and pointed out as Deadman's Lane.   They came again a little later, and burned and sacked the neighbouring town of Rye, which burned so fiercely for five hours that the red glare could be seen far along the coast.   As it has truly been said, the poor people of Rye had a sorry time of it, because of the French; and after the last taking of the town, the inhabitants were so angry, that the mayor and magistrates were all hanged and quartered, because they had not made a better defence.   Unfortunately, the sea, so convenient for those who came from other lands to kill and ravage, never did agree with the place ; for, first, old Winchelsea, built on a low island, was covered by the hungry waves, and then new Winchelsea, built on a hill, with a fine harbour, was deserted and left high and dry by them, so that gradually the once flourishing town became impoverished ; though even when Queen Elizabeth passed through it, in one of her numerous royal progresses, she called it " little London," while, with her

SEA FIGHT OFF THE ENGLISH COAST IN THE THIRTEENTH CENTURY.

asual shrewdness, she warned the inhabitants that the sea was too close for them to be prosperous for long; and so it has happened, for now "little London," once a busy port, is a quaint, silent, over-grown place, though there is not a more interesting spot in all old England, full as it is of ruins of the past.

But perhaps you would like to know more about the Cinque, or five, Ports I so often mention. They are situated along our south-eastern shore, and ever since the time when the Romans took Britain into their hands, and made it a civilised land, they have been under one appointed governor, who is called the "Warden of the Cinque Ports." The five ports are Sandwich, Dover, Hythe, Romney, and Hastings. All these great ports were to furnish war-ships when the king required them—a very important service in those old days. But the constant wash of the waves has so altered the shape of our island, that some of those places which once stood out facing the waves are now far back—Sandwich, for instance, the most northern port, and that used as a frequent landing-place for kings, is now two miles inland; about three hundred years ago the fine harbour began to fill with sand. You have heard, I dare say, of the Revocation of the Edict of Nantes; if not, look for some account of it in your "History," and it will tell you why a very great many French people came flocking to England in the reign of Queen Elizabeth. Very many of these refugees, as they were called, settled in Sandwich, where they cultivated the first market-gardens seen in England.

Edward I. granted great privileges to the lords of the Cinque Ports; for we read that "The barons of the five ports are to be summoned to the King's and Queen's coronation, by writing, forty days before the coronation; and of all the ports there must come thirty-two barons, all in one clothing, and they shall bear the cloth over the King and over the Queen, with four spears of the colour of silver, and four little gilt bells waving above the cloth, which is called the Pall, and shall come from the King's treasury; and at every end each of these four spears shall be attending four barons of the said ports; and the same day these barons shall eat in the King's hall at dinner, at the right hand of the King and Queen." Up to the time of the coronation, the lords of the Cinque Ports always took their places as canopy-bearers in grand array of scarlet and purple feathers and gold chains; but at that ceremony, canopy and bearers were dispensed with, together with many other ancient customs.

From Hampshire, two chains of chalk hills branch off towards the sea, joining the North and South Downs; these extend to a fine rocky headland in Sussex, called Beachy Head, 575 feet high, and the rich and cultivated country between these ridges is called the Valley of the Weald.

Among the clay of the Sussex Weald there are found many fossils and thin beds of limestone, composed of the shells of snails, held together by lime;

BEACHY HEAD.

this, when quarried and well polished, is known as Sussex marble. The tomb of Queen Eleanor, in Westminster Abbey, is made of this; so is the throne of the Archbishops in Canterbury Cathedral, and many other beautiful things in England.

Beachy Head is a fine, wild, rocky place. On and about its cliffs are

"IT WAS SAMPHIRE HE HELD."

countless sea birds and chattering jackdaws. Samphire, a queer little plant,
used as a pickle, flourishes about here; it is often found on steep sea-side rocks,
but never within salt water mark. You may not think this worth telling, and
yet the knowledge of this simple fact once saved four lives; for on a night

when the tempest was raging fiercely, a vessel was wrecked off this very Beachy Head, and four poor sailors were flung on to the ledge of a rock. The tide was rising, the waves were beating furiously, the rocks above were too steep to climb; and the unfortunate men said to each other, "To stay here is certain death, for the tide will soon be up and wash us off; let us throw ourselves back into the sea, on the poor chance of being flung on a safer place." Just as they were consulting, one man almost slipped off the rock, and clutching wildly at a handful of soft green stuff, saw, by the glare of lightning, that it was samphire he held. "Thank God! mates, we are safe," he said, "let us stay where we are, for this is a proof that the tide will not reach us." And so it proved; they were seen and saved next morning.

To the east of Beachy Head extends a deep bay as far as Dover, Pevensey, Hastings, and Battle lying midway. So let us pass on and visit Dover and other parts of Kent.

RECEPTION OF THE EMPEROR SIGISMUND AT DOVER.

DOVER, FROM THE SEA.

DOVER.

WHAT tales these tall white cliffs, only twenty-one miles from the French shores opposite, could tell us of those far-away days we have often read about, when they frowned down upon the steel-clad Roman soldiers, who crowded on their galleys to wonder and stare at them and at the "painted barbarians" thronging along the coast, shaking their rude arms at the invaders, who were fain to pass on further before they ventured to set foot on the little island they had thought to conquer easily.

In the Saxon days, when "Ethelred the Unready" filled the throne, came the Danes, with their dreaded vessels, the terrible "Long Serpents" carved with snakes' heads at the prow, the stern showing the gilt tail of the reptile. Here, later on, the cliffs saw many a boatful of fierce Norse pirates, eager for blood and plunder, and hating the sight of Christians. They were ever ready to burn and slay; but the bold chief Wilfred of Kent had so fortified this part of the coast, that they, too, had to pass on further, and ravage where they could. In time, Dover grew prosperous and wealthy, until in the days of the Confessor it could aid him with the annual service of twenty ships and one-and-twenty men. By-and-by, from over the sea came the steel-clad followers of William, the Norman chief, and as they heard the loud trumpets calling on them to surrender, the citizens of Dover felt their hearts sink within them, and humbly sent their town keys to the dreaded Invader, and bade him welcome, though when he approached, some of the more warlike people and worthy citizens sought to bar his entrance into their unconquered stronghold. But woe to their

KING JOHN BEFORE THE POPE'S LEGATE.

brave hearts! He and his men forced their way into the place, and set it all on fire, leaving only about twenty houses standing, and desolation every-where, to mark their path. After that, when Dover was once more pros-perous, the white cliffs saw many a king and noble pass under their grey shadows into the town. King Stephen died there; and twice there came King Louis of France, on his way to kneel at the hallowed shrine of the famous Thomas à Becket, at Canterbury. Then, too, in the shadow of those same tall cliffs assembled a great army of Englishmen, of all classes, led by that chief whose very name makes our eyes brighten and our cheeks flush, the gallant Richard of the Lion-heart. His white flag, with its red cross, waved above the heads of many whose brave hearts were filled with joyous expectation, but who would never return from that Holy Land whither they were bent to secure the right of Christians to visit the Holy Sepulchre, and to deliver the country from the Saracen yoke. It was on those Barham Downs, overlooking Dover, that King John, the "Lion-hearted's" craven brother, assembled an army of 60,000 men, that he might defy King Philip of France; and there, in the church of the Templars, on the western cliff, he humbled himself, and did submission for his crown before the Pope's legate, and by so doing offended his English subjects and his bold barons so much, that they were ready to accept the prince Louis of France as their king. Dover alone held out against Louis when he came to reign; all the rest of Kent had yielded.

Once, 'tis almost 600 years ago, the cliffs looked down upon a fearful sight, when 15,000 Frenchmen landed and assaulted the town. They grew red with the smoke of burning houses, the blood of women and children; they echoed back the groans and cries of the combatants; but they also saw the fierce invaders driven back, with a fearful loss of life, by a great party of gallant knights, who came shouting their war-cry, and sweeping along, sword in hand, to the rescue of the townsmen.

And see, here is another picture of Dover, in 1216, showing us the Emperor Sigismund, with a gay train of 1,000 horsemen, and a fleet of thirty great ships. He was just preparing to land, when the Duke of Gloucester and divers other lords assembled on the beach, and even entered the water, and with their drawn swords in their hands, refused to let the monarch disembark until he had declared himself their king's friend, and his visit merely that of a mediator to entreat for peace.

Another time, the cliffs, glowing in a gay sunset, saw the landing of the fair French Princess Katharine, bride of our great King Henry V., who, we are told, "was welcomed as if she had been an angel, the people running into the water to carry her ashore on their shoulders."

Just one word about the grand old castle of Dover, of which I will show you a picture. See how it stands high upon a rock, where long, long ago the Romans must have built an "advanced guard," for we can still see the remains of a strong rampart. Britons, Saxons, and Normans

DOVER CASTLE.

have held this place in turn. In the time of William the Conqueror, the defence of the fortress was entrusted to eight of his knights, who held their estates on the tenure of "castle guard," that is, each knight was bound to maintain a certain number of men-at-arms, 112 in all; five-and-twenty at a time to be always on the watch, that no enemies' ships should approach the shore unheeded.

Near the edge of a cliff lies Queen Elizabeth's "pocket-pistol"—it was presented to the queen by the States of Holland—and a very large pocket she would have required for it; for it is twenty-four feet long, and must be charged with fifteen pounds of powder. There is a Flemish inscription on it, which means—

> "O'er hill and dale I throw my ball,
> Breaker, my name, of mound and wall."

About two miles away beyond those green hills lies the tiny deserted-looking village of Guston, or Gorsetown. Near it, in the centre of a dreary field, stands all forlorn the "lone tree," as it is called, and if its withered-looking branches could speak, they might tell a strange weird tale, which perhaps you would like to hear. During the great Civil War, many of Cromwell's soldiers were on guard here in this castle of Dover. Two of them having walked together as far as this field, then smiling and bright with golden gorse, quarrelled, and one, having unluckily a thick branch in his hand, struck his companion on the head, and saw him fall lifeless at his feet. Filled with horror and remorse, he flung the stick from his hand, and fled as fast as his trembling limbs would carry him; but the branch in falling stuck fast in the soft earth, took root, and grew into this lone tree.

To the south-east of Dover lies hilly, crooked, picturesque old Folkestone. There is a fine harbour here, from whence you can embark for the opposite town of Boulogne. I would rather stop on this side the channel, as I am a very bad sailor, and watch the fisher-boats. An old seaman tells me that the Folkestone fishermen had formerly a curious custom, which was to select out of every boat that returned from a fishing expedition eight of the finest whitings that had been caught; the money obtained for these was carefully set aside for a feast, called a "rumbald," which was held on Christmas-eve.

DEAL BOATMAN.

THE GOODWIN SANDS.

AND now, passing on, we cannot go far from Dover and round about our Kentish coast without being soon aware of the Goodwin Sands—

> "Where oft by mariners are shown
> Earl Godwin's castles overthrown,
> And palace roofs, and steeple spires."

They consist of a long irregular line of sands, extending some ten miles from north to south, from Walmer to Broadstairs. Many wrecks annually take place on "this dangerous flat, and fatal," and yet they serve a good purpose as well, for without these sands, the Downs would be impassable in some winds. They form a natural harbour, eight miles long and six wide, stretching between the sands and the shore—where, in 1652, the famous Van Tromp ventured with eighty ships, but only to be defeated by Blake.

I cannot tell you the true story of this place, though tradition has many, which the old sailors love to repeat to their summer visitors out for a view. Some declare that once upon a time, a great feast was given by Earl Godwin upon this island, where then his fair domains stood, and that the castle was crowded with many gay guests, holding high revelry in honour of the wedding of the earl's favourite daughter. All was jollity until the midnight hour, when a furious tempest rose, sweeping all before it into the sea. When the grey morning mist cleared away, the tempest lulled, and the horror-stricken people on the coast opposite looked across, nothing could be seen of the fair little isle—it had disappeared ; only the wild waters and greedy sands, which had overwhelmed and hidden all, were there to tell the tale.

Old Kentish people say that Tenterden steeple was the cause of the Goodwin Sands, and the following is the origin of the saying:—

Bishop Latimer tells us that Sir Thomas More was once sent into Kent on a royal commission, to ascertain the cause of these Goodwin Sands, and the "shelf of sand that stoppeth up Sandwich Haven."

He summoned before him experienced men ; and, among others, came an old man with a white beard, and one that was thought to be over one hundred years old. So Master More called the aged man, and said to him, "Father, tell me, if you can, what is the cause of this great arising of the sands and shelves hereabouts, that stop up Sandwich Haven." "Forsooth, sir !" quoth he, "I am an old man, well nigh a hundred, and I think that Tenterden steeple is the cause of the Goodwin Sands ; for I am an old man, sir, and I remember the building of Tenterden steeple ; and before that steeple was building, there was no manner of flats or sands there."

Now, as Tenterden was a village at some distance, every one laughed at this speech; and yet the old man was perhaps right. For a great many years money had been collected from all the inland people of Kent, to fence in the banks against the sea. Now, this money had always been taken care of by the Bishop of Rochester, and at last, as he found the sea was very quiet, he thought he would use the tax to build a church, with a steeple, at Tenterden ; but as soon as that was done, came a great storm, which brought in the sea with a rush, that destroyed Earl Godwin's island, leaving only a great cruel stretch of sands.

That is one view of the question. But, young readers, I leave you to settle what the steeple could have to do with it, and meanwhile we shall have a peep at the sands as they are to-day. People often go in parties to visit the sands at low water, and even to play cricket on them. You will find that there are three light-ships, beacons, and buoys, to warn mariners of the whereabouts of this dangerous bank, where during a fearful tempest, which lasted fourteen days, no less than thirteen men-of-war were dashed to pieces in the darkness, and their crews all perished. There are usually two men on board the light-ships, which are moored, not by anchors, but by chains, to what are

WRECKED ON THE GOODWIN SANDS

called "mushrooms" (rather tough ones, I fancy), and when a wreck happens in the day-time, two guns are constantly fired, until assistance is seen to arrive. If it is night, rockets are continually sent up in the direction of the wreck, until help is near, most likely in the form of Deal boatmen, noted all the world over. Sometimes there are three or four vessels flung on the sands at one time. One of the men on board a light-ship told me that during a very dreadful gale, he saw a poor fellow washed off the mast of a wreck three times, and twice he was rescued and carried back again by his faithful Newfoundland dog; but the third time both man and dog were drowned, still holding on to each other. After such a storm great flocks of hungry gulls come sweeping round, seeking for what they may devour; they know when a wreck has taken place.

And now something about this Earl Godwin, the father of King Harold. He was once an insignificant person, as we make out from the obscure records of the time. Queen Emma, the mother of Edward the Confessor, was accused by Earl Godwin, whose daughter Edith the king had married, of being accessory to the death of her own son Alfred. The lady loudly declared her innocence, as well as that of Alwyn, Bishop of Winchester, who was accused of being her accomplice in the deed; and what had far more weight in those days, both queen and prelate, to prove the truth, offered to undergo the ordeal by fire. On the day appointed for the trial, we are told that nine red-hot ploughshares were laid on the pavement of Winchester Cathedral, and that the queen and bishop walked over them, before the eyes of all assembled, without suffering the least injury. Of course, they were at once pronounced innocent, and the nine ploughshares were buried in the west cloister of the cathedral. The two who had thus been miraculously preserved, presented, each of them, nine fair manors to the Church as a thanksgiving.

And now, this sad matter being set at rest, the king wondered and pondered who could be the guilty person, and he became suspicious that the same Earl Godwin, who had accused Queen Emma, was the very man who had destroyed her son; but his step-father, Godwin, Earl of Wessex, was great and powerful. And whatever the weak King Edward thought, he determined to hold his peace, the safest thing to do in those troublous times. But the holy festival of Easter (1054) came, and after a solemn high mass in the magnificent cathedral, restored by Alfred the Great, where the bells were rung, and the mass was sung, a great feast was held in the royal city of Winchester. The king, wearing his crown, and his prelates, lords, and courtiers, met in the castle to feast and wassail together, as was the custom of the times. Of course, the great earl and his sons were present in rich and

gorgeous array. Now it happened that the king's butler, in bringing a dish to the royal table, slipped with one foot, and would have fallen on his face, had he not stayed himself with the other foot. "Thus does brother assist brother," cried the gay Earl Godwin, perhaps to give a hint to his own two sons, who were always quarrelling, or perhaps thinking to make those about him laugh at the man's mishap. But a heavy frown and a sad look darkened the brow of the king, who could not resist exclaiming, angrily, "And thus might I now have been assisted by my brother Alfred, if you, Earl Godwin, had not prevented it!"

"Why, O king, do you use these words to me?" cried the startled earl, rising.

REMAINS OF THE OLD PALACE AT WINCHESTER.

A deep and significant silence fell over the gay assembly, and Earl Godwin, looking round, saw many pale and threatening countenances; then he stood up, and holding out the piece of bread he had been about to eat, cried, with a great oath to God, that he hoped it might choke him if he had had anything to do with the murder of the young prince; or, in the quaint language of the times:—"Syr, as I perceyve well it is tolde to the that I

WINCHESTER CATHEDRAL.

shuld be the cause of thy brothere's deth, so mut I safely swalowe this
morsel of brede that I here holde in my hande as I am guyltlesse of the
dede."

"So be it, earl," said the king, repeating a short prayer, as Godwin placed
the morsel in his mouth. Then we are told by tradition that all eyes turned
on him, but swallow the bread he could not; it remained fixed fast in his

throat, and that he fell, blackened and choking, at the Confessor's feet, and was carried out dying by his own two sons, while all present cried, "It is the judgment of God." Oh! if this story be true, as historians tell us it is, what a fearful remorse must have filled the sad king's heart when he thought how he had suspected his own fair mother, and allowed her to pass through that dreadful ordeal, as did the worst criminals of that dark age. No wonder that he turned with horror from the dying earl, bidding them "Carry away that dog, and bury him in the high road." However, that was not done, for the earl was laid in the fair Cathedral of Winchester among his own kindred.

D

KENTISH WILDFLOWERS.

CHERRY-PICKING.

ON OUR WAY—KENT.

SHALL we wander on through Kent—pretty Kent—with its gardens of hops
and cherry-trees, its rich ripe fruits, its sheep, its game, and, above all, its
history? And a right interesting story it could tell, as you will see on your
way, being the county nearest to the Continent, and most convenient for
foreigners to reach our shores. However it may be, invaders of all times
have landed, or tried to land, here; indeed, it is supposed by many, that
long, long ages ago, England was connected with the mainland of Europe by
an isthmus between that part of Kent called Romney Marsh and Boulogne,
in France, where even now the channel which divides the two countries is
shallowest. Once, when Norman Will entered the Kentish village of Swans-

combe, the inhabitants met him in great numbers, and presented a strange appearance, for they all carried immense waving boughs of green trees, and declined to get out of the way until the king had granted them and their descendants several important privileges—such as that of selling their lands when they themselves chose, instead of having to ask their lord's permission to do so, or of dividing them equally among their children, instead of the first-born son receiving all as a right. This custom is called gavel-kind.

The eastern part of this beautiful, fertile "garden of England," is, as perhaps you know, noted for its trim hop-grounds and cherry-orchards—Kentish cherries are famed among fruit. I would like to show you one of these orchards in the fair month of June, when the cherry season commences, bringing together the brown-faced rural population, especially women, of all the hamlets round about. They will be ready for the grain harvest and hop-picking, which will succeed in turn: both cherry-picking and hopping is done mostly by women, each one having a ladder, which is carried about by a man, whose particular duty it is to attend to a certain

HOP-PICKING.

HOPS.

number of these oft-required articles, and to pack the fruit when gathered.

The pretty trees grow in rows, with alleys between wide enough to admit air and sunshine, and some of these grow to be thirty or forty feet high—great mossy wildernesses of green leaves and shining fruit, into which the women scramble, half a dozen busy, perhaps, in each large tree, and they chatter and laugh as they fill the little baskets slung round their waists with the sweet, rosy berries. By-and-by these baskets will be emptied into larger ones, called "sieves," in which they will be sent to market.

And so the work goes on from six o'clock in the morning till tea-time. At noon great fires are lighted, near which the men, women, and children cluster busily; while the dinners are warming, they form separate family parties, under the shady branches, some lying on the grass, some sitting on inverted baskets, forming altogether a pretty, animated scene peculiar to this "garden of England."

Every now and then the mothers come down to look after their babies, for all about the ground tumble crowds of chubby, happy little children, smeared with cherry juice, picking up, and often eating, the over-ripe fruit that falls about them like a sweet bobbing shower.

There are a great many places at which we might stop if time were allowed: the city of Canterbury, for instance, with its quaint old streets and fine cathedral, so celebrated for the martyrdom of Thomas à-Becket, where Saint Augustine first preached, and where King Ethelbert, in the eighth century, built one of the first Christian churches in England.

Of course you all know something of the great story which made Canterbury Cathedral so famous in the old days before the Reformation— the story that brought people crowding from all parts of the world to kneel and pray in Conrad's golden choir, as it was called; to prostrate themselves before a small and simple altar of wood, on which lay a broken sword, a little crystal ball, and a handkerchief stained with blood.

Nothing of this remains, but its story is worth listening to, even if you have heard it before. I will not tell the causes of the struggles for power between a king and an archbishop—that you will find out if you turn to your History and read the reign of Henry II.—I will only figure an irritated monarch, so harassed and angered by his rebellious subjects as to exclaim publicly, "Of the cowards who eat my bread, is there not one who will free me from this turbulent priest?"

The priest, Thomas à-Becket, was Primate of Canterbury, with power and will to ban and curse the enemies of the Church of Rome, which he represented. He had lately returned from a long exile in France, proud and angry, yet to all appearances reconciled to the king, who mistrusted him. The king spoke in his anger, but his rash words fell on too ready ears, as a wish, almost an order, that the archbishop should be disposed of. So, quickly arming themselves, four of his knights hurried off to England, and having arrived at Saltwood Castle, there, in the darkness of a long winter's night, they laid their plans, and in the morning they issued orders, in the king's name, for a troop of soldiers to march with them to Canterbury; then they rode away as fast as their horses could carry them along what is called Stone Street, a road which runs in almost a straight line of fifteen miles from Saltwood to Canterbury.

The next day, as the archbishop sat in his own apartments after dinner, he was informed that four knights, three of whom had been in his own service, had come in hot haste to confer with him. Stern and gloomy, they entered and sat down, scarcely noticing the salute or answering the greeting with which they were received. They looked sullen and threatening, and curtly ordered the primate, in the king's name, to leave England for ever. " That I will not do; never again shall the sea lie between me and my church. How dare you threaten me in my own house?" he asked, confronting them with dignity. "We dare do more than threaten, Sir Priest, and shall return expecting to find you gone," cried the knights, threateningly, as they withdrew. "Come when you will, you will still find me here," said the prelate, as he saw them depart.

But a cold chill of terror fell over that priestly company—only à-Becket sat cool and collected, until the sweet sounds of evening-song and service rose in the chapel near. He knew his peril, but he feared it not, or, rather, prepared to meet it in a manner befitting his high office and dignity. So the time passed on, until one, aroused by the sound of chanting, cried eagerly, " To the church! to the church!" The primate refused to fly, even though by this time he knew that the knights and soldiers had returned fully armed, and were, sword in hand, forcing their way in; they could even now be heard breaking down all before them with their battle-axes. Then the half-frantic monks and attendants about à-Becket dragged him off, in spite of all resistance, through the cloister and into the church. They struggled, and quickly closed and barred the door against the furious assassins, already in sight.

A strange, sad scene it must have been on that dismal December evening, where, amid the gloom that enwrapped arch and pillar, the tall and fearless archbishop, followed by his attendants, walked up to his favourite altar, and hearing the shouts, and cries, and curses of the knights without, ordered them to be admitted, saying that God's house should not be made into a fortress in his defence. Then almost all those who had brought à-Becket hither fled and hid themselves in dismay ; but he turned bravely to meet the doom he too plainly felt was near ; attired in cloak and hood, he stood with his back leaning against a column between the altars of St. Mary and St. Bennet.

In rushed the four knights with twelve soldiers behind them, and the dim altar-lights twinkled upon flashing drawn swords and flushed and angry faces, whereon could be read no mercy for that unarmed man. Foremost through the shadows came one Hugh of Horsey, shouting, "Where is the traitor ? where is the traitor ?"

Only a profound silence followed. He cried again, "Where is the archbishop ?" Then à-Becket's voice rose clear and thrilling, "Here I am, the archbishop, but no traitor." Soon followed a scene of wild confusion, of threats and recriminations, a scene which ended in darkness and bloodshed, which I care not to remember and describe. For though the murderers would fain have dragged their victim from the sanctuary he had sought, in this they failed, as one true priest threw his arms round the archbishop's waist, and held him back, and when a blow was aimed at à-Becket's head, swiftly interposed his own arm, which was broken, I believe, by that very sword which was found on the spot ; but all in vain, for other blows came thick and fast, and soon the victim fell, his hands clasped, and his mantle wrapped round him. His last words were, "For the name of Jesus and the defence of the Church I am willing to die."

Then, in the silence that followed, that guilty band looked on each other with pale faces, then turned to fly—to ride away to a place of safety, in the darkness of a fearful storm which broke over the city.

Out from their hiding-places crept the horrified monks, gathering round the fallen prelate, lying so calm and still in the shadow of Conrad's choir. When the news of the murder reached King Henry, in Normandy, where he was keeping his Christmas feast, it is said that he received them with the greatest sorrow and distress. After some time, à-Becket being canonised, or pronounced a saint—whose remains were capable of working miracles—many persons, rich and poor, gentle and simple, came from all parts to visit his shrine and relics—so many that "the Canterbury pilgrimages" became quite celebrated. Chaucer, the old poet, says that—

CANTERBURY.

CANTERBURY CATHEDRAL.

" Bishops and abbots, priors and parsons,
  Earls and barons, and many knights thereto ;
  Sergeants and squires, and husbandmen enow,
  And simple men of the land,"

came every year. There were extra-grand pilgrimages every fiftieth year
for the next three centuries, and in 1520, the year of the last jubilee, King
Henry VIII. and the Emperor Charles V. rode under the same golden canopy
through the streets of Canterbury to worship at the shrine of St. Thomas.
But soon came the Reformation, and all this was ended, through the means of

this very King Henry, who, perhaps, was tempted by the jewels and gold he saw piled on the rich altar or decking the robes of the priests of St. Thomas.

But besides this story that we are reminded of at every turn in the church, the town has one of its own, which is well worth remembering; for it is the oldest home of Christianity in England, though in the great "once upon a time," when Saxon and Dane ruled the land, only pagan temples stood where now crowd spires and pinnacles.

Here it was that that brave Roman, Augustine, and his pious band of missionaries, came to visit and convert the pagan King Ethelbert and his warlike but ignorant people. At that time Canterbury (although the Saxons had named it Cantwarabyrig, "the stronghold of the Kentish men") was only a rude, timber-built city, embosomed in thickets, and must have seemed very shabby and unimportant to the Roman visitors, as they approached in procession, bearing aloft the cross of Christ, and chanting a solemn litany. So they came down St. Martin's Hill, and entered Canterbury, and with them came the first glorious light of Christianity; for soon, influenced by his wife, the pious French Princess Bertha, Ethelbert listened to Augustine's teaching. He allowed him and his to worship openly, and, in the end, was publicly baptised—a good example, which was followed by ten thousand of his subjects on the Christmas Day following; not in a church, as there was not one yet, but in the river Swale, flowing so conveniently near.

After that the missionary work prospered. There is a ruined arch still shown which is thought to be part of the church of St. Pancras, the first one dedicated by St. Augustine. It had, before this time, been a heathen temple, and a wonderful tale is told concerning some rough marks on it, which are *said* to be those of a demon that clutched it and tried to shake it down on the occasion of the first Christian service held within. Other churches were consecrated to the service of God, and in the end Ethelbert even gave up his own palace, and an old temple adjoining it, in which to hold a house of prayer, and retired to Reculvers, near the sea; there he dwelt in another palace which he built himself with the ruins of an old Roman fortress. It seems very strange, as we look at the present stately cathedral, to think that it stands on the very site where stood a pagan temple so long ago.

Very slowly the city rose to fame and importance, but it did rise to its own destruction for a time; for being conveniently near the islands of Thanet and Sheppy, the landing-place of the fierce Norse rovers, it was continually being attacked and plundered, and at last, in one desperate raid, the town and its inhabitants were almost entirely destroyed by fire and sword.

Long years after this, in the days of William the Conqueror, we find Canterbury again flourishing, for the Norman Bishop Lanfranc took it in hand, pulled down the ruins of the ancient timber church of St. Augustine, and raised a grand new stone one in its stead. He spent seven years in the good work, which was afterwards further improved and beautified by his successors, until at last it was finally dedicated to the Holy Trinity, with a splendour and magnificence which (if we are to believe an eye-witness) was never surpassed since the days of the dedication of Solomon's Temple.

There are so many splendid monuments in this grand old church that we cannot spare time to do more than just peep at one that you young people will be specially interested in—that of the famous hero of Crecy and Poitiers, Edward the Black Prince, who always favoured the city in which he desired to be buried. There lies his effigy, once gilded to look like an image of solid gold, in full armour; his handsome head resting on his helmet; his hands, which had so often wielded a victorious sword, now joined in humble prayer. Above are suspended the gauntlets, the helmet, and the wooden shield; even the velvet coat he wore, once emblazoned with the arms of France and England, now hangs here, all tattered and faded; there is the empty scabbard which held the good sword of the brave warrior, whose motto, "Ich dien," "I serve," and the three feathers so familiar to us, is carved all about the handsome tomb, which is fashioned after his own design.

One other tomb we must notice is that of another famous hero, Henry IV. and his fair wife Joanna. I believe that all the archbishops up to the Reformation are buried here. Some of the monuments are exceedingly curious; we may not stay to describe them, as it would fill all this volume.

ROOM IN HEVER CASTLE.

HEVER CASTLE.

And now for a glance at another place in Kent, which also has its story. It is a building—half castle, half mansion—still in very good preservation, enclosed in a large stone courtyard, and surrounded by a deep moat. There are fine gardens around it, and altogether it is a brave place; and here for generations lived the family of the Boleyns—whose name reminds us at once of England's Bluff King Hal, who chose one of its daughters for a wife, most unfortunately for her, as we all know.

We can wander through the quaint rooms, some of them so little changed in appearance since the days when the "Brown Girl" sat thinking of her royal lover and her chance of being Queen of England, or, maybe, watching at the large bay window in the Long Gallery as the gay hawking-party assembled below, laughing merrily at some pleasant joke or the sudden flutter of some eager bird held up for her admiration, or listening all expectant for the bugle of watchmen stationed on the hills ready to announce the approach of the gay crowd—the monarch and his courtiers galloping in all haste from London to head the merry chase. The grand old oriel window is still there, and the pleasant chamber, with its carved oak panelling, its fire-dogs, even to the same heavy chairs and tables. But when we look at them they

ANCIENT FURNITURE AT HEVER CASTLE.

remind us how swiftly pleasant days passed away, and how the fair young girl, now crowned Queen of England, and now a disgraced prisoner, must have remembered the peaceful, happy hours she had spent at Hever, in the stately gardens of which she was first seen by the king, and which, after her death, were seized upon by her hard-hearted husband, and presented to his third wife, the Lady Anne of Cleves, who, in turn, lived and died there.

Penshurst, on the Medway, is where the good and great Sir Philip Sydney lived in the days of Queen Elizabeth. The furniture here is very quaint and old. In one room the embroidery is said to have been the work of the busy queen and her maidens.

WEST DOOR OF ROCHESTER CATHEDRAL.

ROCHESTER.

Rochester is an interesting old town, with a castle which is said to be the finest specimen of Norman architecture in England, and a cathedral still very beautiful, but that has suffered much from time and still more from man.

Under the castle wall, where the broken, time-worn stones are overgrown with creeping plants and ivy, there is a pretty walk, commanding a view of the Medway and the green fields and uplands on the opposite side. Adjoining Rochester is Chatham, and here this river is very deep.

During our wars with the Dutch, their admiral, De Ruyter, determined to

ROCHESTER CASTLE.

make an attack upon the English dockyards, knowing they were in a weak and unprepared state. Soon he came with seventy big men-of-war, and many a dangerous fire-ship, and boldly made a descent on Sheerness, carrying off sixteen iron guns and a great heap of war stores, which caused such a panic in London, that, we are told, "everybody was flying none knew why or whither, and the wealthier citizens buried their gold and jewels for safety sake, in case the Dutchmen came so far."   The Dutch sailed up the glittering Medway, broke the boom, and set fire to the guard vessels

DE RUYTER'S ATTACK ON UPNOR CASTLE.

moored behind it.   Then six men-of-war and five fire-ships came to destroy Upnor Castle, but here they met with such stout and determined resistance, that they sailed back again, burning and destroying many ships on their way, and among others, the *Royal Oak*, whose brave old commander, Captain Douglas, declared that a Douglas was never known to leave his ship without orders, and so went down with his ill-fated vessel.

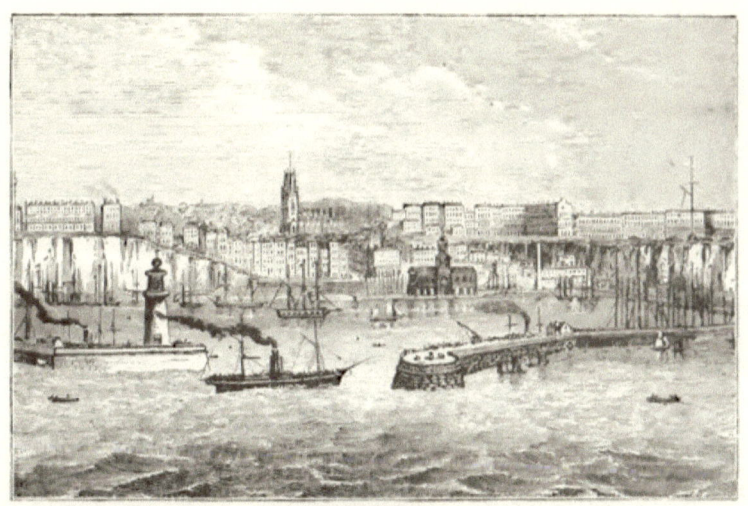

RAMSGATE HARBOUR.

THANET.

" Ramsgate herrings, Peter's lings,
Broadstairs scrubs, and Margate kings."—*Old Saying.*

THOSE of you who have spent a holiday on that corner of Kent, called the Isle of Thanet, may not know that it is so named from a Saxon word, meaning a fire or beacon, probably because of the many beacons or watch-fires lighted to give warning of the approach of enemies to fair England's coast—

" To tell that the ships of the Danes,
And the red-haired spoilers, were nigh."

The Saxons, or Jutes, held Thanet as an all-important position, and the remains of one of their largest cemeteries has been discovered near Ramsgate. It is nine miles long, and eight miles broad. South of Ramsgate is Pegwell Bay, said to be the place where Hengist and Horsa landed on their visit to Britain.

In old days all this coast, like that of Sussex, was famous, or rather infamous, for its wreckers and bold smugglers ; now it is peaceful enough

E

MARGATE.

to be crowded with summer visitors—papa and mamma rest under the shadows
of the cliffs, while boys and girls dance about on the soft yellow sands, or
rush on to the pier to watch for new arrivals.   An old writer says—

> " Soon as thou gettest within the pier,
>   All Margate will be out to crow ;
> And people rush from far and near,
>   As if thou hadst wild beasts to show."

But perhaps this was written in the times when it took three days and
nights to travel to Margate, in what was called a "hoy ;" now we get
there in about six hours by steamer, and in about three by rail—so much for
the power of steam.

Near Margate is quiet, pitchy Broadstairs, with its honest, brown-faced
boatmen, and its troops of little visitors.   Here, once upon a time, there was

an image of Our Lady of Broadstairs, held in such reverence by mariners, that every ship that sailed by lowered its topsails in its honour. Now I think we are more interested in the place because Dickens lived there, and that it possesses a pretty asylum for motherless children.

Along this coast you will see three fine lighthouses, standing on the great chalky cliffs of the North and South Foreland and the tongue of land known as Dungeness—three important places. Everywhere the pretty yellow sea-poppy flourishes bravely among the swamp and shingle.

South of the Isle of Thanet, a little further along the Kentish coast, and approaching Deal, we come to Walmer, the *Sea Wall*, opposite which begin the Goodwin Sands. In the old churchyard here, it is thought that Cæsar fought his first battle; and there are many remains of ancient encampments. The great Duke of Wellington, who was warden and guardian, or Lord of the Cinque Ports, died in its castle. There may be seen the little bed-room in which he slept, on a narrow iron bedstead and hard mattress—no self-indulgence for the brave old soldier, who used to say, that when a man wanted to turn in bed, it was time for him to turn out of it. He himself always rose at six, and could often be seen thus early pacing the castle ramparts ; but in 1852 his watch ended.

> " No more, surveying, with an eye impartial,
>   The long line of the coast,
> Shall the gaunt figure of the old field-marshal
>   Be seen upon his post."

WALMER CASTLE.

A ROCK-BOUND COAST.

ABOUT LIGHTHOUSES.

PERHAPS, having seen the outside of a lighthouse, you would like to have a peep at the interior of the North Foreland; see, there it is on a hill! The glass-house, or lanthorn, on the top, has what we may call great glass eyes, one glaring up-channel, the other down-channel, while the glare of the two together can be seen far out at sea.

Let us knock at this door, and show our order for seeing over the place; then we go up a stone staircase—up, up, up—the stairs becoming narrower as we near the top.

"Hush—sh!" murmurs our guide, warning us not to make any noise as we pass the room where the head light-keeper is soundly sleeping, in preparation for his next lonely watch. "Hush—sh!" as on we go—softly, pit-pat, up the narrow spiral staircase leading to the light-room at the summit of the tower.

Here we are at last, on a broad landing-place; then up a few more steps, then at a door, then in a small chamber, so full of glowing light it might hold the enchanted diamonds of some proud monarch of the "Arabian Nights."

See, the well-guarded jewels are placed upon a semicircular platform of bright copper; and, as we look in, we see the back part of the apparatus on which they are arranged in a double row. Talk of diamonds shining as these do, though no diamonds after all! "These centres of light" look very like lamps, each having a glass chimney over it, and a large round reflector behind it, a huge metal dish with a shining silver face — bright enough to dazzle the sight out of our eyes, as we pass directly in front of them, feeling like small black flies in the intense glare, and glad to get out of it. We try to stare about us on a little balcony, and through a small window of thick plate-glass. We cannot see much—all is so dark outside, but are startled by the sudden flop of a bird against the glass. Poor thing! it is a gull, that has stunned its head against this

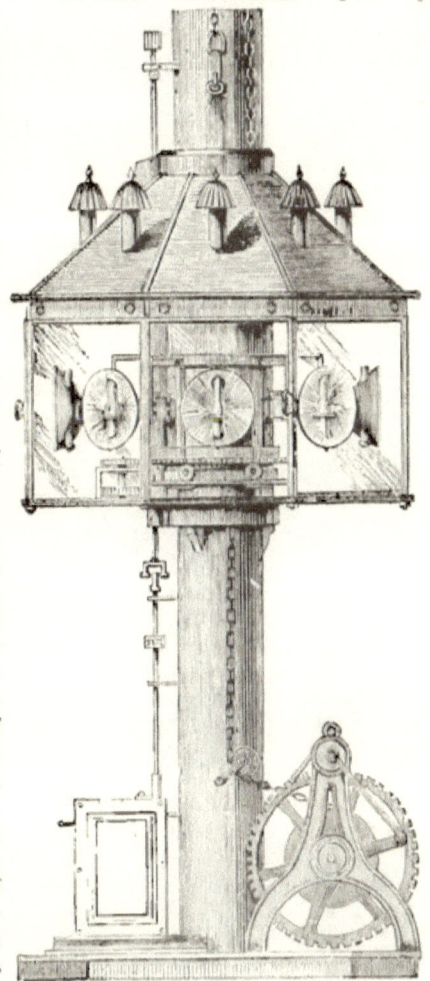

REFLECTORS AND WORKING APPARATUS.

hard glass with its fascinating glare, for it has very much the same effect on birds as a candle has upon a poor dazed moth that *has* to go headlong in it. The keeper tells us that he often finds dozens of birds lying stunned or dead in the balcony.

Then we go down, down, down the narrow staircase, thinking over the strange, silent, orderly scene we have just left.

The keeper tells us that each great shining reflector increases the

NORTH FORELAND LIGHTHOUSE FIFTY YEARS AGO.

effect of a fixed light, usually an Argand lamp, three hundred and fifty times; and the larger ones, used for revolving lights, about four hundred and fifty times, though, of course, it depends upon the distance at which they are observed.

This system, called the "catoptric," of lighting our dangerous coast is divided into nine kinds; and as some of you may be living by the sea and able to watch these fiery signals on a dark night, I will tell you a little about their working, that you may be all the more interested in them.

The fixed lights need no explanation. The revolving lights you know well, if you have ever looked out seaward on a starless night, and seen first a dull light, which brightens and fades, to gleam again in a few minutes. This effect is produced by the revolution of a frame, with three or four sides, having reflectors ranged on each. The succession of red and white lights is, of course, caused by the revolving frame presenting lamps of a different colour as it turns.

The flashing light is produced in the same manner as the revolving light; the difference is in the arrangement of the mirrors or reflectors, and especially in the greater quickness of the revolution, or turn, of the frame, which gives the effect of a sudden flash over the waters once in about five seconds; then comes the intermittent light, which bursts suddenly on us, shines steadily, then as suddenly disappears for a time. Coloured lights cannot be seen at as great a distance as white ones, and are only used by way of necessity. Next to the white in power is red; if you notice you will see that green and blue are seldom used, except in pier and harbour lights.

In some dangerous places, where there is no possibility of erecting lighthouses, we find light-ships, or floating lights. These are really large lanterns of copper framework and plate-glass, covered with wirework, hung at a mast head. Within the lantern are placed, perhaps, eight Argand lamps and reflectors, helping to cast their warning rays over the rock or cruel sand-bank.

Even the building of a lighthouse may have its story. Do you know that of the one on the dangerous Eddystone rocks, which lie some nine miles from the coast of Cornwall? First of all, Mr. Winstanley built a timber one, not unlike a Chinese pagoda, but though the lantern rose sixty feet above the rock, the waves rose higher still, and soon mastered the light. Then the builder heightened the tower to a hundred and twenty feet, but that was too much, and when wild windy weather came, it was very much injured. Folks said it was not safe, but Mr. Winstanley had such confidence in his work, that he declared he hoped he should be in it during a storm; and, strangely enough, it soon happened that, being in the lighthouse overseeing some repairs, a fearful storm did arise, and the angry winds and waves roared and beat against its sides, lashing it in their fury, until they swept the tall tower away, and with it brave Winstanley and his workers, who were thus buried in the wild waters they had tried so long to resist.

Then, all round about the cruel Eddystone, half hidden in the waves, the wild winds roared, and many a brave vessel was wrecked for want of the warning light.

SMEATON'S LIGHTHOUSE ON THE EDDYSTONE.

Soon another tall tower was built by John Rudyerd, of London. It was all of timber, and ninety feet high; again the beacon light shone bright and steady over the waves; but one unlucky day, just a hundred years ago, the timber caught fire, and the whole building was burnt down to the water's edge, and there was once more an end to the Eddystone Lighthouse.

Then came John Smeaton, and laid the foundations of another lighthouse; and he set about it in the most practical manner, and with great ingenuity, cutting the surface of the rock into a regular flat foundation, likely to support any weight. The first twelve feet of the tower formed a solid mass of masonry; altogether it stood sixty-eight feet high, and was formed on the principle of the stem of a tree. This stood firm for very many years, but gradually the rock on which it was built was undermined by the sea, and it became necessary to erect a new lighthouse.

Another lighthouse I should like to show you is that on the Incheape, or Bell Rock, though I must remind you it is on the Scotch not the English coast. Do you remember Southey's verses, "Sir Ralph the Rover?" Here, in olden times, so many vessels were wrecked that the abbot of Aberbrothock did really cause a float, having a large bell attached to it, to be so hung, that the motion of the waves should cause a constant tolling. Then beacon after beacon was erected and washed away; and at last Robert Stephenson, the great engineer, set to work A difficult task it must have been; for, as the rock was only dry for a few hours at spring tides, the men had constantly to retreat to a vessel moored off it, and once the thirty-one men and Mr. Stephenson were almost lost by the tide suddenly rising, and the vessel breaking adrift. But at last the lighthouse was completed, and it now stands firm and strong, and a hundred feet high. Its door is reached by means of a massive bronze ladder; and in calm weather we may often row by and watch the keepers on the look-out for some of the many dainty fish to be caught hereabouts. If it be night, look up at the light—it is revolving, red and white, caused by the revolution of a frame containing sixteen Argand lamps and their reflectors. The machine that turns the frame can also, when the weather is foggy, cause two large bells to toll. A strange sight and sound it must be on a dark night: those large red and white eyes peeping out of the gloom one after the other, and the slow boom, boom of the warning bell, heard so steadily sounding above the roar of the wind and the splashing of the sea, reminding us of the good abbot.

THE LIFEBOAT ON ITS CARRIAGE.

THE LIFEBOAT

" THE lifeboat ! the lifeboat ! when tempests are dark,
  She 's the beacon of hope to the foundering bark ;
  When, 'midst the wild roar of the hurricane's sweep,
  The minute-guns boom like a knell o'er the deep.

" The lifeboat ! the lifeboat ! the whirlwind and rain
  And white-crested breakers oppose her in vain ;
  Her crew are resolved, and her timbers are staunch ;
  She 's the vessel of mercy, good speed to her launch !

" The life-boat ! the lifeboat ! now fearless and free,
  She wins her bold course o'er the wide rolling sea ;
  She bounds o'er the surges with a gallant disdain,
  She has stemmed them before, and she 'll stem them again.

> "The lifeboat! the lifeboat! she's manned by the brave,
>   In the noblest of causes commissioned to save;
>   What heart but has thrilled at the seaman's distress,
>   At the lifeboat's endeavours, the lifeboat's success!"

I HAVE been to see a lifeboat launched: truly a pleasant, I had almost said a holy, sight on this shining summer's morning, when the water ripples so softly on the yellow beach. It is a pretty boat, gaily painted, and drawn on its carriage by eight sturdy horses, and followed by a lively procession of sea-side folk—sailors' children, big boys, little boys, and visitors, who have hurried from their dinner to watch the sight. See, there is a fair, blushing lady, dressed all in white; she is to christen the boat. Watch her stand up, holding that bottle of wine, which is hanging by a cord to the lifeboat; she gives it a sudden hard rap on the boat's side; smash! it goes; she calls out a name—the "Faith," I think it is, but the people shout and cheer so, I cannot be sure. While the horses rattle the odd carriage down nearer to the sea, there is another louder hurrah! And with one long run on the shingle, and splash into the sea, the lifeboat is launched, and may fortune attend its good work for many years to come!

As I told you, many of the people who dwelt round about our coast watched with anxious interest when a storm drove a disabled vessel to the sea-shore. They were not wondering if they could save life, not they; indeed, they preferred letting the poor shipwrecked traveller perish without help, lest they should claim as theirs anything that might be cast on land, or that might be saved from the wreck. Instead of help, lights were often placed in dangerous places; and often, when the poor sailor thought he had at last reached a place of safety, he was put to death by wretches who took possession of his ship, and plundered it in the storm and darkness.

But now, thank God! all this is changed, and instead of these miserable people, there are bold, brave men, who watch in a storm for far different reasons—they are ready to risk their lives to save poor drowning people, and instead of false signals to lure ships to destruction, they boldly man the lifeboat, and venture on the foaming waves.

In the reign of Charles II. we find some slight mention of a lifeboat, but for a long time they were very scarce and unsuitable; and all kinds of vessels were dashed to pieces, one after another, within full view of the people on land—sometimes friends and relations of those on board, who had no means of going to their assistance, even if they felt inclined to do so. As in the case of the *Adventurer*, stranded just outside Tynemouth Haven, the unfortunate crew could be seen climbing up into the shrouds for safety, and could plainly be heard crying for help which no one could give them ; and, though great

AT THE MERCY OF THE WAVES.

rewards were offered by the authorities, all the poor men were drowned in broad daylight, while thousands of people were looking helplessly on.

Then people began to think something must be planned to save wrecked men from such a dreadful death ; and at last a Mr. Greathead invented a splendid lifeboat, which could toss about in the heaviest sea and never be upset. This was first launched in 1790 ; and Government gave this benefactor of his species twelve hundred pounds, and the Emperor of Russia sent him a splendid diamond ring--presents well deserved, you will say. Since that time, many improvements and alterations have been made in these useful little craft; and now, almost all round the coast, there is a house on the

TO THE RESCUE.

beach, in which is a lifeboat, mounted on a machine that easily runs it to the sea, from whence willing hands as easily launch it. As soon as that fearful cry is heard, by day or by night, "A wreck! A wreck!" the lieutenant of the

THE DEPARTURE.

THE RETURN.

lifeboat assembles his men, who hastily take their places in the boat, horses are fastened to the machine, and by some special contrivance, the little vessel (usually painted white, or striped blue and red, to catch the eye of those on board the wreck) is swiftly launched, and away on her mission of mercy. The work is full of peril—for sometimes the boat is dashed against the wreck, or against rocks, and all on board lost ; but little the men think of their own danger.

I will just tell you, in a few words, what a lifeboat usually is like. I have used a picture of one, so you can see for yourselves. It is about thirty feet long, and ten wide, and is alike at each end, so that it may dash through the waves either end foremost. It generally has five seats for rowers, and is manned by ten oars. It is cased and lined with cork, four inches thick, and secured with plates of copper and copper nails, which makes it so buoyant, that it will float all right, even when it has been very much dashed about in a violent sea. At the bottom of the boat there is a heavy iron keel, to prevent its being upset. Sometimes the boats fill with water, but they scarcely ever sink. The crew wear cork jackets and life-belts filled with cork, and take life-buoys with them, to be all ready. These are large round casings filled with cork, which can be slipped over a man's head and shoulders, and which keep him from drowning ; cork will not sink, as you can easily test by floating a small piece in a cup of water.

Sometimes people are taken off a sinking ship by means of rockets—things somewhat like the fireworks boys send up on the 5th of November. This rocket consists of a case full of gunpowder, with a stick at the end of it. To this stick is fastened a long and strong rope. When the rocket is fired, the men on shore keep fast hold of one end of the rope, while the men on the wreck try to catch the other end which is fastened to the rocket-stick, which, it is hoped, will fall somewhere on board the ship. This joined, gives them a line of rope from the ship to the beach, and by this they may escape, though you most likely wonder how they cross so frail a bridge, with the wild waves dashing madly over and around it ; surely the frightened people must drop off. But no, it is a simple matter after all ; for a big basket is made to slip along the rope by means of a line, which, by using another rocket, is sent from the shore ; then one end of this line is held by the men on land, and the other by the men on the ship, so that the basket can be pulled and slipped backwards and forwards along the rope, each time, perhaps, saving a man, woman, or child from a fearful death. Truly all this is a great advance on the old days.

Notice, before we quite lose sight of Ramsgate, the fine harbour, built by Smeaton, the same man who built the famous Eddystone Lighthouse. In old days, this part of our coast was quite celebrated for the many fearful wrecks that annually took place about it; and when it was decided to put there a harbour and lighthouse, the lord of the place petitioned Government that it might not be done, in justice to him, as a great part of his income was derived from the vessels dashed to pieces or stranded on this dangerous beach—a curious plea, which, fortunately, was not attended to. So now travellers by sea need no longer dread, as in times of old,

> " Those Kentish men that dwell upon the shore,
> Look out when storms arise and billows roar,
> Devoutly praying, with uplifted hands,
> That some well-laden ship may strike the sands,
> To whose rich cargo they may make pretence."

DIVERS AT WORK.

A CHAT ABOUT DIVERS.

How strange it is to think that deep down in the waters of the sea is a mysterious world, not level as one might expect, judging from the rippling surface, and the smooth, sandy beach shining in the sun; but so uneven, that (as one tells us, who sounded the sea along the route for the first Atlantic cable) in it there are places where Mont Blanc—the great white mountain of the Alps—whose summit is three miles above the sea level, might be sunk without showing even its peak above water.

Much of what we call mud at the bottom of the sea is soft chalk, in which creep countless tiny insects. In some parts, great reeds and twining plants cluster round wrecked ships, and in the warm south these grow where the sun shines brightest, the reeds and plants become great trees, forests of foliage through which strange fishes gaily swim, as the birds fly up in our world.

How can we know what this fairy realm is like, you ask, when to visit it is death to poor mortals? Not always, for there are beings that go down into these depths unhurt, that breathe, eat, and walk, perfectly safe and comfortable. Strange creatures they are, huge monsters, in fact, much bigger than you or me—strangely ugly too. They have stiff, hard, shiny heads, queerly shaped, and great, goggle, glassy eyes; and see, they breathe through very long tails which spring from the back of their ugly heads—are they fish, or goblins of the deep?

Though they do all their work in the sea, they have no regular dwelling-places there, yet somehow they are found in queer dangling houses without floors, in which they sit working dry and unconcerned. Now, do you guess what these strange creatures are, or must I tell you more?

Divers, of course! There are a good many about our coast. Perhaps some of you may have seen them—a busy set; they are, as a rule, masons or carpenters; many of them make plenty of money by mending the hulks of steamers to save them from sinking. But the principal work of a diver is to recover lost treasures. By his aid a sunken vessel can be searched from stern to prow, and everything cleared off as thoroughly as though she lay high and dry on the beach. For instance, after the *Royal Charter* was wrecked some years ago, divers went down to see what they could find, and one man came upon a massive bar of gold, worth I cannot tell how much, besides other treasures. When the *Great Eastern* steamship was returning from her first trip to America, she sprang a leak below the water-line and began to fill, and had not a diver gone down and patched her up at once, the costly vessel would have sunk for ever. Another time, during the war with Russia, the great war steamer *Agamemnon* was shot through below the water-line, and would have gone down with all on board had not the carpenter, who had once been a diver, fortunately happened to have preserved his armour. This he instantly put on, and while the cannon balls flew splashing about him, sprang bravely into the sea, reached the side of the vessel, stopped up the holes, and so saved his comrades' lives, and the good ship from sinking.

Of course you all know that there are men in Ceylon, Africa, and other parts of the world who dive for pearls and sponges. This is known to have been a practice long ages ago. These natural divers, as I must call them, using just a little framework to bring up their prizes on, and sticking a knife between their teeth to keep off hungry sharks, go down simply holding on to a rope.

But in Europe it is a different thing ; and besides a diving-dress or armour, made of india-rubber, with a helmet of leather and metal, men go down in a diving-bell—a simple invention enough, which I can perhaps make you understand by an old experiment of filling a tub with water, then floating a lighted taper, stuck in a cork, on its surface. If you take a clean dry tumbler and hold it over the light, you will find that you can press it down, downward to the bottom, the light still burning, and the tumbler empty and dry within. But in a short time the light will go out for want of fresh air, just as a man's life would do, if, instead of a taper and glass, you put a man under a huge bell. So to remedy this, a pump is used, that is constantly worked, forcing fresh air in and bad air out. If you have visited the Polytechnic, you have probably seen a splendid bell at work, and you may have gone down in it, if you have had a fancy for experiments. I have been told that the first sensation is a very unpleasant one—something like having a swarm of bees humming inside your head. If you fancy trying on a diving-dress, you will have to get into it as you would into a sack, as it is all in one piece from the neck downwards. The helmet is screwed on afterwards, like the top on a smelling-bottle.

As it is not very easy to keep up a conversation in a diving-bell, there are a certain set of signals used. The diver cannot hear the men at the pump, but those in the open air can hear him, and when he wants more air, he strikes one blow on the side of the bell and they pump faster. If he wants to be drawn up, he strikes three blows; and so on. Or if it is any unusual message, he uses small coloured buoys, or even writes on a piece of wood; these being set free from the bell, float to the surface of the water, and are caught up by those on the look-out.

AT PLAY ON THE SANDS.

This talk about diving reminds me of the pleasant yarns of Mr. Wood, late landlord of the "Diver's Arms," a roadside inn facing the sea, at that little watering-place, Herne Bay, in Kent. Some of you young people may have been there for a summer's holiday, and noticed it when frolicking on the beach, digging treasures out of the sands, or sitting on the steps of the rather stiff-looking clock-tower, just opposite the house I mean.

This William Wood was just the man to gossip with on such matters, for he had been a diver for nearly thirty years ; and he loved to talk of those old times, and even to show a mass of thin worn-out-looking Spanish dollars, which, along with others, he had picked up from their bed in the deep blue sea, where they had lain hidden for many and many a year. Indeed, that same sea had been a kind of fortunate purse to him, so he had good reason to speak of it kindly. Shall I repeat the story of those very dollars he was so fond of telling about ?

Have you ever heard of the Copeland Islands ? You will find them on your map of Ireland. Well, in years long gone by, it was said that many accidents befell the vessels that came this way ; and that once, during a dreadful storm, a very large ship, laden with slaves and Spanish dollars, was dashed to pieces in the night. The poor slaves, fettered and manacled, sank at once, but the owners of the dollars tried hard to save themselves, and might, perhaps, have succeeded, but they could not leave their darling dollars behind, and tucked them in their pockets, and in their sleeves even, so that when they tried to scramble up the bleak rocks, the weight of the silver dragged them down again into the hungry waters ; and in the morning no one would have known what had happened in the darkness, had it not been for the pitiful waving of those weighted hands as the tide went down, the sea looking so calm and still now its cruel work was finished.

This tale, often told by the simple people of the island, who, on stormy nights, would declare that they heard the clink of silver and the rattle of chains, was heard and pondered over by a thoughtful English coastguardsman, who, remembering his own friends at Whitstable, where lived several well-known divers, wondered whether, in case the tale were true, it would be possible to find any of these silver dollars that were thought to be lying somewhere at the foot of the wave-washed rocks. It might be worth the venture, he decided ; and so he wrote to his old chum, William Wood, and told him the whole story. And he and others, ever ready to seek in the waters for things likely or unlikely, determined to start on what some folk called a mere wild-goose chase. But little our few friends cared, as they gaily sailed away from English Whitstable to Irish Donaghadee—they believed in luck and pluck, as Englishmen generally do, and well was their venture repaid, as you will see.

I dare say the few people who gathered round to watch them make their first attempt were rather horrified when they saw them don these strange, unearthly-looking suits, and thought them mad when, thus cumbered, they were lowered into the sea. But this gave our divers little concern as they marched about on the rough ground, searching, feeling, peering for some sign of the fabled

A TREASURE TROVE.

treasures. It was light enough deep down under water to see strange things, of rock, and leaf, and grotto. They startled lazy wondering fish, that flapped hurriedly away from these strange, hideous intruders; they poked their heavy crowbars into many a nook and cranny, seeking for treasure, but nothing could they find ; no merry jingle of silver repaid their trouble and labour. For many hours they searched, feeling with their hands around rocks and crevices ; they wandered about in that wonder-land over deep weeds, and tangle, and broken shells and sand ; until at last, when they had begun to despair, one man lighted on a mass of unusual form, and bringing up a lump of it into the broad daylight, found that it was the rusted remains of iron handcuffs, which, no doubt, had once held together the wrists of some miserable slave.   The story was true so far, then, and on closer search more manacles were found ; then at last dollars—silver dollars, by twos and threes ; then by masses; some which had been once enclosed in a barrel were still matted together in the same form, though the hoops and the staves were gone.

And so our joyful and enterprising divers continued their work in right good earnest, and brought up the long-buried money in rusty-looking heaps. Many of the pieces were so mixed up with sand and stones that the men took down shovels and sieves, and riddled them out at the bottom of the sea, just as the gardener sifts out the gravel.   They were thin and worn with the action of the waves, but still they were silver dollars, which they brought up, some all soddened together in lumps and clusters—dollars to the value of many thousand pounds. Well might they rejoice, those lucky Whitstable men ! for when their work was done they found they had cleared over five thousand pounds ; and as, I suppose, William Wood had had enough of the sea, he devoted his share to the purchase of the "Diver's Arms," at Herne Bay, where I heard this story.

"But didn't you feel afraid sometimes down there, master?" and I pointed to the blue waters opposite the house.

"Afraid ! no !" he laughed.   "If any one is afraid he would not do for a diver, I can assure you of that."

Then he told me many anecdotes ; among others, how the fish would generally dart away in horror when he came floundering down among them ; but sometimes they would appear more curious than frightened, and come back after a while, and swim about in a state of great wonderment.

"One day," he said, "a big old lobster chose to be angry at what he evidently considered an invasion of his domains, and sat staring out of a cranny in some rocks, exactly where the diver wanted to work.   There was no getting him to move ; there he waited, with his great black claws and pincers all ready for a spiteful nip, as soon as he should get a chance ;

so at last a long iron crowbar was lowered by a rope and pointed at him. At this he made a ferocious snap, and, taking it for an enemy, held on like grim death, while, on a signal being given, the men above hauled up their crowbar, and before he knew where he was, Mr. Lobster went flying through the water, still holding on to his victim, and soon, I have no doubt, served his captors as a meal."

Another time, when a diver was resting quietly on a rock, a great shoal of pretty whitings came dashing up against this moveless visitor. They seemed very much interested in the big glass eyes, and tried hard to swim through or to bite them, so next time he was lowered he took a fish-hook on a stick with him, and when they came dash up against him, he caught some, and hung them to his waist-belt, for his supper.

Herne Bay takes its name from the pretty village of Herne (Saxon— "nook or corner"), about two miles inland, where there is an old church, of which the celebrated Bishop Ridley was vicar. There is also a fragment of the gateway of Forde Palace, where bluff King Hal visited Cranmer, and where Cranmer and Ridley revised the Articles of the Church of England. Altogether it is a "nook" worth visiting, though I expect you children will prefer a frolic on the fine sands.

WHITSTABLE.

WHITSTABLE.

" The oyster loves the dredger's song,
For it comes of a gentle kind."

TALKING of Whitstable divers reminds me of Whitstable itself, a little town which lies in a sandy bay, and seems to consist of a long row of cottage houses, and a fish-like smell. It is all filled with prosperous fishermen, for here is one of the principal farms in England, not a farm for fruit and cabbages, as you might expect, but for oysters—"real natives"—which are collected here in great water-beds, reared from the time they are only "spat," to that other time when they are carefully taken up and packed for the London market, where they fetch a great price.

As English oysters have always been a delicacy, it is said they brought the Romans to our shores in days of old, and as Whitstable is particularly famous for them, let us linger here, and learn a little of the doings of the blue-eyed fisher-folk who live and work in these happy fishing-grounds.

OYSTER-DREDGING.

The flourishing oyster-beds here belong to a company that keeps up a large fleet of boats for the purpose of dredging and planting the beds. It is an old and honourable company, into which no strangers can enter, as a member must be a born dredgman—no money can buy him the distinction ;

and when he dies his interest dies with him, but his widow will be provided for, and have one-third of her husband's income allowed her. The oysters all require the greatest care, from the tiniest one, called "brood," the size of a threepenny-piece, which is dredged up by dredgers in boats, or by men who collect it when the tide is ebbing. They do not grow fast, and they have many enemies; but if carefully tended, in about four years a bushel of "brood" will have grown into about five bushels of valuable "natives." Every year each layer of oysters is examined day by day, so that the state of almost each individual oyster is seen. The men have good regular wages, but they are only allowed to dredge for three months in the year, the rest of the time they have to attend to the fishing-grounds, keep them clean, and clear away mud, insects, and any oyster enemies that may creep in; for the oyster has many foes—sea-crabs, for instance, that would soon drill a hole in his back, or hungry star-fishes, that are said to hug the oyster, and force him to open that he may be swallowed up.

THE DREDGER'S IMPLEMENTS.

LOWESTOFT.

THE EAST COAST.

BUT if we want to see the busiest fishing town "round-about," we must go on and on in a northerly direction, until we come to Norfolk, a county washed north and east by the raging restless waves, which supply the people with plenty of fish, especially herrings. Who has not heard of Yarmouth herrings? The pretty silvery things come swimming round about this coast in great shining shoals, to be caught and carried to Yarmouth, the largest sea-port in the county. This odd-shaped, fishy-smelling old place, built on a strip of land between the river and the sea, is not unlike a gridiron, with its five long streets stretching from north to south, and its hundred and fifty-six narrow alleys crossing it from east to west.

Of course, you have all heard of Yarmouth Bloaters ; they are a cheap dainty, celebrated all the world over. In the charter of the town, it is required that a hundred herrings should annually be sent free to the sheriffs of Norwich, who are to have them made into twenty-four pies, and then forward them to the Queen or King of England.

Before it reaches Yarmouth, the Yare expands into a great sheet of water, which at times looks like a lake. Close to Yarmouth are great dangerous sand-banks, constantly changing their shapes; and which are, I need hardly say, a source of great peril to the many ships that sail along that part of the coast.   On the beach several " Look-outs" have been built, from which you can get a look-out of all the ships in the Yarmouth Roads, these roads consisting of a passage of deep water between the shore and the

HERRING FISHING.

sandbanks, which do not rise to a level with the water.   On these sand-banks are moored light-ships to warn mariners in stormy weather of their dangerous presence.

Far out at sea we may watch the herring-boats coming in laden with many thousand silvery fish.   As it is said that our English fisheries produce somewhere about £60,000,000, we might as well take some notice of them, especially of the herring, as it is the greatest prize of all.   Their great numbers have made whole nations prosperous ; to the Dutch they have proved a mine of wealth. It is their "great fishery." Whaling is "the small fishery," and in the olden time it is often mentioned in history. The curing of herrings was discovered by Benkel, a Dutch fisherman. Two hundred years after his death, the Emperor Charles V. solemnly, and in great state, ate a herring on Benkel's tomb, in honour of the poor man who had done his country so great a service. We read that in 1195 the city of Dunwich, Suffolk, was obliged by charter to furnish the king with 24,000 herrings. There was "a pretty dish to set before a king!" Let us hope he was fond of them.

Have you ever noticed the deep blue colour along the back of this

THE HERRING.

pretty fish? When it is alive it is just like green-ish metal, and on it there are strange odd markings, which look almost like letters, and the fisher-men used to believe that these were really words in some unknown language. Three hundred years ago, two herrings were taken on the coast of Norway, which had such peculiar marks that they were carried to the King, Frederick II. The prince looked well at the signs, and turned white with fear ; he thought he read there an omen of misfortune or death. He sent all round his kingdom for learned men to aid him to decipher the warning ; and together they made out the words, " You soon will cease to fish herrings, as well as other people." Great was their consternation ; and when the king died, a year afterwards, most people thought those innocent herrings were celestial messengers sent to bid the king prepare for death. But to return to boats. A Yarmouth boat is a decked vessel costing £1,000; smaller boats leave her with one hand on board while the rest of the men go out and fish. How laden they are, and how glad the blue-eyed fisher's children will be; and no wonder, for father has signalled that the haul has been a good one, and that means comfort at home. This fishery is regulated by Act of Parliament, and the meshes of the great draught net, made of fine twine, are all to be of an inch square, that the smaller fish may fall back into the sea, and grow bigger before they are again caught.

FATHER'S BOAT.

Come now for a peep round about Suffolk, with its many farms, its sheep, horses, and prize pigs. It adjoins Norfolk, as you know; and this part of England was once all called East Anglia—the people who lived in the north being called "North-folk," and those of the south, "South-folk." This county is said to be the best cultivated in England.

A SUFFOLK FARM-HOUSE.

There are many narrow rivers flowing about here, and near their mouths they widen to form little arms of the sea, so plenty of fish is to be had, especially mackerel and sprats. Two of these rivers are called the Linnet and the Larke; and on the Larke stands the ancient town of Bury St. Edmunds, about which I can tell you a quaint old tradition.

Lodbrog, the Danish prince, was, like most great folks of his time,

G

very fond of "hawking;" and one day, while enjoying his favourite sport, one of his most valued birds fell into the sea. Anxious to save his pet, the prince, without pausing to look round for aid, and only followed by his greyhound, leaped into the first empty boat he saw, and hastily put off to try and rescue it; but a sudden strong wind blew, a storm arose, and the little boat was tossed along and across the raging sea, up the mouth of the Yare—Yare-mouth—and after many perils, the prince was flung on to the coast of Reedham, in Suffolk, and there, having told

THE DANISH PRINCE AND HIS HAWK.

his name and dignity, the noble Lodbrog was well received, and taken to the brave and pious Edmund, King of the East Angles, who, as it happened, held his court within a short distance, being then at the royal palace of Thetford, which had been a British city before the days of the Romans, and near which is Keminghall, where Queen Boadicea once held her court.

Edmund received the royal Dane in right princely fashion, treating him with all kindness and respect; and finding that he was excessively fond of hawking, gave him dogs, and his own head falconer as an attendant, when he should feel inclined to indulge in the sport. His skill and success in it filled the English king and all the courtiers with admiration—all but Bern, the king's falconer, whose heart filled with envy and jealousy against the skilful new-comer who

threw all his own doings in the shade; so that one day, when he was alone
with him in the dark woods, he treacherously shot him, and buried him
under the green ferns, and heaped up leaves and brambles over his grave,
thinking that he could easily declare that Lodbrog had thought proper to go
off alone, and that he, the poor falconer, had asked no questions.

And so all passed off quietly for some days, though this sudden absence
puzzled not a few; but what soon puzzled them more was that they also
noticed that the stranger's greyhound came home for food every now and
then, quickly departing as soon as its wants were satisfied. It whined, and
seemed in trouble; at last it was followed, and the poor creature led the
attendants straight to the place where its murdered master's body lay hid in
the depths of the forest.

There was a great stir and consternation among the dwellers in the old
palace when this sad tale was told. Bern, the falconer, was interrogated, and
the dog, being brought into his presence, growled and tried to fly at him and
to tear him to pieces. All things pointed him out as the murderer, and he
was condemned by the king, in the strange retributive fashion of the times,
to be turned adrift alone, without oars or sail, in the same small boat which
had brought the unfortunate Lodbrog to meet his death on our shores.

But, stranger still, the little skiff was wafted back safely to the Danish
shores, and at once recognised as a native-made boat, and the very one in
which their king had gone adrift. Bern was seized, and carried in haste
before the two princes—Ingnar and Hubba—the sons of the late king, who
anxiously questioned him about their missing father.

The wicked falconer, fearing lest his own crime might be suspected, coolly
replied that the king had certainly arrived at the English coast and court,
but that he had been put to death by King Edmund's command.

On hearing this, the grieved and enraged princes resolved on revenge,
and at once raised an immense army to invade the dominions of poor
innocent, unsuspecting King Edmund. These fierce Norsemen soon landed
at Berwick-upon-Tweed, killing and burning all before them, and marched
forward, intent on vengeance, until they reached Thetford, then King Edmund's capital, which the princes seized upon, and there beheaded the king,
who refused to buy his life by denying his faith, and whose head was thrown
in a thicket, where tradition says—*I* don't, mind—that it was preserved by
a grey wolf, that kept guard over it until it was found by some of his

distressed subjects, who carried it back, quietly followed by the now tame animal, and that it there and then joined itself to the body again. The remains, considered to be those of a saint and martyr, were long afterwards laid in a church at Beoderickworth, which afterwards became celebrated as Bury St. Edmunds, a sumptuous monastery having been founded there by King Canute. Of this little trace now remains, beyond the gateway, for it was ravaged and destroyed in the civil wars.

Journeying along the coast, we pass many towns and villages, thriving farm-houses, and remains of ancient fortresses, past the old Roman castle of Burgh, supposed to have been built in the days of the apostles ; at last we reach the town of Lowestoft, the most eastern point of all England, and a famous place for a dip in the blue sea. Then on past many a quiet fishing-village and sleepy hamlet, until close to the beach, near to Dunwich, now a tiny, insignificant place, once a very large and important town. Then there was a wood standing, which extended a mile and a half between the town and the sea ; but its trees have long lain far under the advancing waters, that washing ever onwards, first undermined and swept away the cliffs, then had easy mastery over houses, churches, monasteries, and flourishing gardens, leaving nothing but sand and shingle in their room.

THE GARDENS OF OSBORNE HOUSE.

ISLE OF WIGHT.

LET us go for a change of scene to the pleasant and flourishing Isle of Wight, separated from the mainland of Hampshire by the roadstead of Spithead. We must cross the beautiful Solent in a steamer, though it is said that in the times when the Phœnicians traded with Britain for tin—and you know it was that very trading that made our land known to the civilised world—the channel could be crossed by men and carts at low water, which, unlikely as it looks now, may have been possible in those early days, seeing how much the shape of our coast has altered in the course of time. To those who understand all the wonders told by layers of clays, and chalks, and sands, this island is particularly interesting. But where shall we begin? At Oysterbourne, or Osborne, where our Queen often spends her holidays? she has loved it from the days when as a little princess she lived there with her mother, learning her lessons and dressing her dolls like any other little girl. Or at Ventnor, with its wonderful Under-cliff? Or, rather, at pretty, green Bonchurch, where fuchsias and passion-flowers grow every-where? Yes, we shall begin with Bonchurch, for it reminds us of the story of a brave-hearted sailor lad, named Hobson, who lived in the days of good Queen Anne. This boy, it is said, was born at Bonchurch, and losing both his parents, soon became—much against his inclination, for he wanted to go to sea—an apprentice to a friendly tailor at Niton, a village near by. There were often wars and rumours of wars in those times; and one day, when a squadron of great big vessels, real "hearts of oak," went gaily round Dunose in pursuit of the enemy, and a crowd of villagers, masters and men, all left their work, to go rushing madly through the quiet streets and along the yellow beach cheering and hallooing, young Hobson ran with the rest, and not only ran, but somehow managed to run right into a boat, and row to the admiral's ship, and offer himself as a cabin-boy, or anything they would have him for. Few questions were asked, as an engagement was expected to come off soon, and all the men who would come were welcome. So the youth once on board, the boat floated back to the beach with only young Hobson's hat in it; and those who found it there thought that the orphan apprentice was drowned, and all because poor Hobby had not stuck to his needle and thread—as the old folks said.

Almost the very next day, the English squadron encountered a French one, and the battle began fast and furious, for both were terribly in earnest.

"Please, sir, how long will this fine stir last?" asked the new cabin-boy, of a brown-skinned, bare-headed old Jack tar, coming rushing by with a great load of gunpowder in his strong arms, which were tattooed with many a strange shape, as is the fashion with many "old salts."

"How long will it last, you young land-lubber? Why, till that white rag yonder," pointing to the white flag at the enemy's mast-head, "has struck to us English. So get out of my way, we've hot work before us!"

"HOT WORK."

"Oh, well, if that's all, I'll go and see what I can do towards bringing the row to an end," was the laughing answer. And the tailor's apprentice darted off unheeded into the midst of a red mass of fire and smoke, where seamen, French and English, were engaged in a deadly encounter, hand to hand.

During the struggle the ships had got close together, roaring, rattling, shaking against each other, yard-arm to yard-arm. The fray grew desperate and doubtful; but no one observed that a lad had climbed up the rigging, and regardless of bullets flying in every direction around him, crossed over to the French ship, and quietly removed the white flag, which was waving defiantly in the breeze.

Suddenly some English sailors, seeing the enemy's flag gone, and taking this as a token of submission, shouted joyously, "Victory! victory!" The startled Frenchmen stopped firing, and even left their guns in surprise and dismay, and their ships were boarded and taken before their defenders had recovered from their confusion or understood their mistake.

When comparative quietness had been restored, young Hobson, the cabin-boy, came slipping down the rigging, and unconcernedly made his appearance on the deck, with the large white flag carelessly wound round his arm. That was an English lad's way of "doing what he could."

For this deed of daring he was at once promoted to a better position, and by other acts as bold he soon rose to be an admiral, and was ere long knighted by Queen Anne.

One bright summer's day, long afterwards, when the old tailor of Niton was busy stitching on his shop-board, there arose a great stir in the village streets, and a gay party of officers, all in blue cloth and gold lace, knocked at the cottage-door and begged of the tailor's wife to oblige them with some dinner, as they were strangers and hungry, and would be glad of a rest.

"But indeed, gentlemen," said the good woman, all in a flutter of astonishment, "I have nothing to offer you. Times are hard, and I was just cooking our own plain dinner of eggs and bacon. I could not set such common fare before you, though, of course, if you will, you are welcome."

But the officers declared that there was no dainty dish they could have preferred to eggs and bacon; and they all sat down to dine, and laughed, and seemed to enjoy the meal very much—all except one, the best-dressed and the handsomest, and he fidgeted up and down, and asked many strange questions about the past. At last he pushed his plate aside, and began to sing the first verse of a quaint old song. The old tailor got up and stared at him, all of a flutter; the old tailor's wife hid her face in her check apron, and began to sob.

"Oh, please, don't sing that! Hobby, my poor drowned Hobby! 'tis the very song the dear boy used to be so fond of; I cannot bear to hear it again; please don't sing that, sir."

Then the delighted admiral took both her hands in his own, and kissed her, saying that he was the poor runaway boy who had plagued her so, and for whom she had grieved so long. And I should not like to declare that there were not tears in other eyes brighter than the good woman's, or to believe that times were quite so hard after that in the humble cottage that had sheltered the youth of brave Vice-Admiral Sir Thomas Hobson.

I cannot visit the Isle of Wight without telling you one or two other stories connected with the fine old castle of which I have shown you a picture.

In the good old days, when "might was right," the Norman King William I. seized on the then strong fortress, and bestowed it upon one of his favourite knights, William Fitz, son of Osbert; and here that valiant lord and his compeers held many a gay revel—inviting guests from all the country round, where many a Norman dependant held estates of the "Honour of Carisbrook." But in time the warlike Fitz Osbert died, sword in hand, and face to foe, as became a Norman knight. Count Rodger, his son, considering he had many wrongs, took up arms and rebelled against the king —a dangerous experiment, as he found to his cost; for soon his estates were seized upon, and he himself, hidden in some deep dungeon, was heard of no more.

Now, as you may have read in your English history, this stern King William had a brother, who, as was the fashion of those early and warlike times, was half-priest (Bishop of Bayeux) and half-soldier (Earl of Kent). He was powerful, and rich, and ambitious—much loved and trusted by the king, who, when he decided once more to visit his own dear home and vineyards in Normandy, left Sir Odo behind him in great state and prosperity; little thinking that the selfish, ungrateful prelate would soon set about collecting a large body of fighting men at this fortified castle.

But some loyal bird carried a warning of treachery over the sea, and King William, ever ready to face the foe, returned in hot haste, having instantly summoned his vassals and men-at-arms to meet him at Carisbrook immediately; and hither they came trooping, from far and near, to find their monarch seated in state in that royal hall, where the brothers soon met face to face, by the bright light of hundreds of torches that shone on steel armour and silk embroidery.

CARISBROOK CASTLE.

"What shall be done to this man, this subject—so base, vile, and treacherous, that he would fain betray his king and brother, his trust, his adopted country? Answer me this!" inquired William, pointing at Odo, and sternly turning to the awed and silent crowd of armed men around. All fell back; their frowning faces spoke their thoughts, but Odo, the vengeful, proud warrior-priest, was too dangerous for them to dare to irritate or to molest. No one ventured to answer, or accuse such a one as he.

"Seize him, guards!" shouted the imperious William; but no one stirred —no one moved—on so dangerous an errand.

"Seize him, I say; he is a traitor! Do ye not hear, cravens?" Then as all drew back affrighted, the king himself sprang from his chair of state, and caught the proud bishop's embroidered sleeve; but Odo, calm and sullen, shook him off, saying, "Sir, I am a priest! none but the Pope has a right to judge me, whatever I am accused of."

"Right," answered his brother, sternly. "I may not punish the priest, but I can disgrace the base noble I have made;" and he himself handed over the Earl of Kent to his guards. And Odo was sent far beyond the sea, and imprisoned for years in a lonely Norman fortress; while William, his brother, ruled in fair England.

Long years after this, in 1377, a large party of French sea-rovers landed on the island, and travelling over hill and dale, at last encamped before the walls of Carisbrook; but the old fortress was strong and well defended. The besiegers, not well armed, and unacquainted with the place, were defeated and destroyed, not one returning to his own country to tell of the failure of the expedition, which was to have made their fortunes—an expedition not uncommon in those days. The country people still point out the Noddies' or Simpletons' Hill, as the place where this happened.

And now we come to the days when Charles I. was king, and the great civil war began. Then the castle was garrisoned with royal troops; and it being considered a safe place, the Countess of Portland, wife of the governor of the island, and her five children, were entrusted to their care, under the charge of the brave Colonel Brett. But the people of Newport were fierce Parliamentarians, and, aided by soldiers, besieged the grey old fortress. The king's garrison, few in number, held out as long as they thought possible, and then, disheartened and nigh starving, began to talk of surrendering. The enemy outside would make no conditions, or give any promises of mercy; and it would have gone hard with those loyal fellows who, after all, had only done their duty to their master and the lady in their charge, had not the brave countess herself rushed upon the ramparts, and with a lighted torch in her hand, declared, in a loud and unfaltering voice, that, unless these men, the king's servants, were allowed to surrender on honourable terms, with life, and limb, and liberty, she would herself fire the powder; and when they did gain possession, Parliament would own only a mass of ruins. The besiegers,

KING CHARLES I.

filled with wonder and admiration, granted the terms the noble and determined lady dictated, and Carisbrook Castle was safe once more.

THE KING BROUGHT TO CARISBROOK CASTLE.

In his youth Prince Charles had hunted, free, happy, and respected,
in the glades of Parkhurst and Carisbrook ; but now civil war raged all
over England, and there came a day when this same King Charles I. was
brought, in bitterness and disappointment of heart, to dwell in this stern .

fortress, at first as lord and master, with a revenue of £15,000, crowned, sceptred, but powerless as king, and very soon treated as a forlorn prisoner. It is said that he tried hard to escape from the cage in which he had been so sternly barred by his subjects. At one time, especially, everything was splendidly planned; even a horse, all saddled and bridled, led by a faithful cavalier, was ready, within a stone's throw of the castle, to lead the captive to where anxious, waiting friends had a boat all manned and ready to sail for France, to bear their king once more to liberty and power, maybe a throne, again; only, what seemed one little difficulty to be surmounted, Charles must get through his chamber-window. The doors were too well guarded for any other chance of egress; and, unluckily, the deep-set windows proved just a little too small for the poor anxious monarch to squeeze through, and so he had to stay within. Another time he managed to remove the bars, but was detected. The guide will still tell the story, and point out the "King's Window."

At length Charles really did leave the castle and the fair island, being roused up in the darkness of a December night, and hurried off by a detachment of Parliamentary soldiers, who carried him to Hurst Castle, on the other side of the water. The last we hear of him is, "that, in the year of our Lord God, 1649, Kinge Charles was beheaded at Whitehall Gate." In one of his books at Carisbrook he had written these words, in Latin:—

> "In evil times, life we may well disdain;
> He doeth bravely who can suffer pain."

Soon after the king's departure, came hither some very innocent prisoners, namely, his two poor children—Princess Elizabeth, "a lady of excellent parts, great observation, and an early understanding," a fair, sweet maiden of fourteen, and her brother, the boy Duke of Gloucester, a bright, strong lad, who flourished in spite of gloomy walls, and stern-faced sentinels watchfully guarding his every step. But as for the young princess, poor girl! thinking of the dearly-loved father, who had so lately died, his last words bidding her ever forgive their enemies, even as he forgave them, unnoted and uncared for, she faded and drooped day by day. She never repined, but, with sweet words of resignation and trust, waited for the time when she might rejoin in heaven the tender father she had so dearly loved on earth. She was weary and sick, and untended; but, as she did not complain, perhaps those about her scarce knew

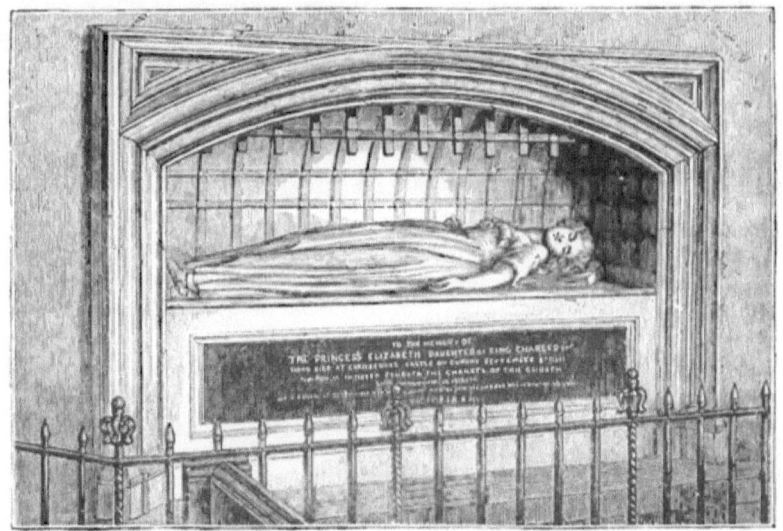

MONUMENT TO THE PRINCESS ELIZABETH.

how weary and sick the child was, or believed her in no danger; until that bright September morning, when the pitying sun, glancing in at the little window to cheer the helpless prisoner, found her, with a smile on her lips, and her patient young head resting lovingly on the pages of an open Bible, her father's last and cherished gift. He had told her "that it had been his constant companion through all his sorrows, and he trusted it would be hers." And so, indeed, it had been, as all about her knew. But now she needed no words of promise or comfort, no earthly sun to cheer her sad eyes; she had left the grim old castle prison-walls for ever; dark looks and ungentle words were all far, far behind, as far as earth is from heaven; and soon the silent, sorrowful attendants had laid her in the chancel of St. Thomas's Church, at Newport, without either royal pomp or even religious ceremony, marking her humble grave with a stone, on which were the initials " E. S."

And thus all thought of the ill-fated child of an English king soon passed

THE WELL AT CARISBROOK.

away; and her sad story might have been altogether forgotten, had not our own dear Queen Victoria heard it, and caused a monument in memory of the princess to be erected. If we enter Newport Church, we shall see the beautiful white marble monument, with no gilding or finery about it, but consisting simply of the graceful figure of a fair young girl, carved in pure white marble, and lying, as tradition says the princess was found, with her head on the Book of Life, with the simple epitaph inscribed :—

"TO THE MEMORY OF THE PRINCESS ELIZABETH,
DAUGHTER OF KING CHARLES I."

And so I end my sad but o'er-true tale.

I cannot leave these ruins without taking you up the seventy-two broken steps that lead to the old Saxon keep, or down again into the shed where is the castle well, which, in ancient days of siege and warfare, was one of the most important places. That patient old donkey has been trotting in and out of the wheel winding up a bucket for the last twenty years; no wonder he knows exactly how many turns to go, or trots off the moment it is at the right height for those little people to get a cool drink. The well is at least two hundred feet deep, and this Neddy works precisely as did the "turnspit dogs" in the olden times, before coal fires were general in England.

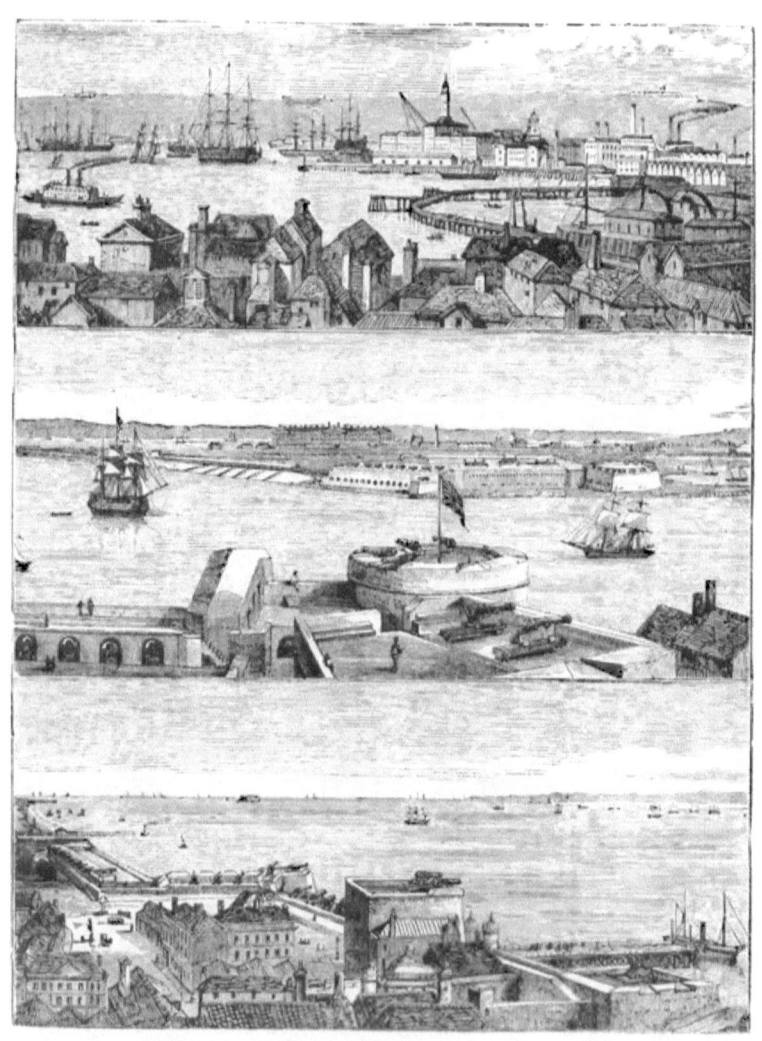

PORTSMOUTH—THE HARBOUR—THE FORT—STEAMBOAT PIER.

IN THE NEW FOREST.

HAMPSHIRE.

THE very name of Hampshire, the mainland opposite the Isle of Wight, reminds one of the days when William had it cleared with fire and sword that he might enjoy the royal sport of hunting. The New Forest lies between Southampton Water and the Avon. See, here is Portsmouth, the chief naval arsenal in England, where the largest man-of-war can be harboured in safety. Here lies the old " Victory," on which Nelson was killed. Every 21st of October the ship is garlanded with laurel, to remind us of the victory of Trafalgar.

We cannot pass Winchester by unnoticed, for it is one of the most ancient towns in all England. It has been said that it may possibly have existed, as a village in the woods, for a thousand years before the

Christian era, flourishing before all others in story and tradition.   In the "once upon a time," when the Romans ruled, they enclosed the city in massive walls of flint and mortar, as we see it to this day, and erected temples to Concord and Apollo on the site of the present church.

But after the Romans withdrew from Britain, troubles and tribulation swept through the land, and at last the Saxons became its masters. Soon the warlike Cerdic, the founder of the West Saxon kingdom, came sweeping down upon Hampshire, defeated the Britons, and even captured Caer Gwent, turning its cathedral into a heathen temple, where the Saxon gods were worshipped, and altering its name into the Saxon word, Wintanceaster.

But though all its art and commerce seemed crushed and gone for ever, Wintanceaster was still the chief city of the most powerful king of the island ; and Cerdic, having resolved to declare himself monarch of the western kingdom, assembled his chief subjects, and was crowned in the new Pagan Temple of Thor—so lately the cathedral church of the Christians.

But Christianity revived in time, and as though to make amends for its apparent downfall, our famous and favourite king, Alfred the Great, was born at Winchester, was trained within the ancient walls of the cathedral, once more restored to their ancient purpose under the care of the celebrated Bishop St. Swithin ; and here he rested at last in the new minster he had built for himself and family. It was in this cathedral that Queen Emma walked over the nine ploughshares ; and here that Earl Godwin, her persecutor, was buried. Later on, when the Normans came, Winchester was still regarded as a "royal city," where kings were crowned, and where laws and measures were passed.

When William I. became king, he and his looked upon all Saxon buildings with contempt ; and Bishop Walkelin undertook, at his own sole expense, to rebuild the cathedral of Winchester. But soon timber ran short, and the Conqueror gave the bishop liberty to cut down and carry away as much timber from the royal forest of Hampinges, near Winchester, as he could in three days. The bishop finding that he should require a great deal of wood, quickly collected all the woodmen he could find in the county, and setting them to work, managed, by promises and threats, to make them cut down every tree in the forest, and to carry them all off within the given time. The king soon passing that way, missed his fair green forest. It was gone—not a tree left. It might have been the work of wizard or fay, so neatly was it done, and so impossible did it seem.

"What does this mean?" cried William, rubbing his eyes; "am I mad? certainly I had a beautiful wood here but the other day! What can have become of it?"

INTERIOR OF WINCHESTER CATHEDRAL, SHOWING NORMAN AND GOTHIC WORK.

When he discovered the trick, he was very angry at first, and refused to see the bishop. However, after a time he forgave him, saying, "Assuredly, Walkelin, I was too liberal in my grant, and thou too exacting in the use thou madest of it." So the building of the cathedral went on, though it was eight years before service was again held in it.

It was while hunting in the neighbouring forest, that William Rufus

DEATH OF WILLIAM RUFUS AT STONEY CROSS.

was shot by his own bow-bearer, and brought back to Winchester in a dirty charcoal cart, to be buried in the choir of the cathedral, "many people looking on, few grieving," as old records tell.

In later times the city was gay with the royal courts of many princes; there were fair palaces and flourishing monasteries. The castle was once besieged by King Stephen, who wanted to get possession of Queen Maud; but she caused herself to be carried out of the fortress, fastened up, as though dead, in a leaden coffin, and so escaped from his clutches.

Even the City Cross of Winchester could tell its tale—how in the old persecuting times a poor Dutchman, who had been brought before the warder for reading his Dutch Bible, was sentenced to be led by the town-crier round the cross three times with the Bible in his hand, and then back to the market-place, where the book was to be flung into the fire, and the Dutchman to be taken to prison.

One of the things that make the city more "royal," to my mind, is that the great primate, William de Wykeham, was born there. I must not linger to tell you of all the good things he did; how he built and endowed two famous colleges at Winchester and Oxford; and at last, after a life spent in good deeds, was buried in the old cathedral, which is still one of the finest buildings in England.

The thing my young readers would feel most interested in is the painted table of King Arthur, constructed by the enchanter Merlin, at which, tradition tells us, he sat with his knights, each place equal in honour. It is a large oaken slab, on one side of which is painted a royal figure, wearing a crown; round it there are names and inscriptions painted in old black letter. It is very curious and interesting; but I am afraid that great King Arthur never saw or sat at it, as it is really not so old as some like to imagine; but then folk even say that there never was a real King Arthur, that his story is that of many brave knights rolled into one. But I like to believe in him, don't you? as we so often hear about him in our visits to old places, especially in the West of England.

Near Winchester is Wolvesly Castle, which is interesting, because here it was that, in the year 951, King Edgar ordered a tribute of 300 wolves' heads to be brought to him annually, and accepted wolves' tongues instead of money fines for offences. You may be quite sure that our English wolves had little chance of their lives after that proclamation.

In the old times, before hotels for the accommodation of travellers were thought of, the many pilgrims, men and women, who came to our coast to visit the great shrines of Canterbury, Winchester, Chichester, and others, were accommodated at what were called "hospitals," the word having a very different meaning from what it has in our day. A hospital was called "Maison

Dieu," or " Domus Dei," that is, "God's house," and was generally founded
at a seaport town, or near the sea, to accommodate the pilgrims. There was
a Domus Dei at Southampton, and also at Portsmouth, Dover, Arundel, and
other places. They usually united the entertainment of travellers with the
care of the sick, and were generally built within the town walls, that they
might be within the reach of the ailing; for in those days the brethren were,
as a rule, the only persons who understood the art of medicine and surgery.

As it is well to learn all we can in our wanderings
about England, we will just peep at the hospital of St.
Cross, near Winchester, which, by some strange chance,
escaped the destruction that fell on other such establish-
ments in the stormy days of the Reformation.

At this Domus Dei, founded by a brother of King
Stephen, thirteen poor men were to reside and be cared
for, each one to have daily a loaf weighing three pounds,
a gallon and a half of small beer, a good dish of meat,
and a mess of milk and wastel-bread—that is, of the
pure white bread that was only made for nobles. But
that was not all; for every day there was a table spread
for a hundred poor folk, who gathered from all parts.
The room in which they fed, now used as a brew-house, is
still pointed out, and called, "The Hundred Men's Hall."

Later on, Cardinal Beaufort rebuilt part of it, and
gave a great sum of money, so that thirty-five reduced

PILGRIM, 13TH CENTURY. gentlemen should be admitted to reside in the old hospital, which he called the "Almshouse of Noble Poverty." Although
parts of this old building have been destroyed or pulled down, to this
day thirteen poor brethren (who each possess three small cells, and a
garden), with a master, steward, and chaplain, still reside here, and doles of
bread are distributed to the poor of the neighbourhood on certain days
—a practice which carries us back to the days of monks and friars and
baronial halls. A piece of bread and a horn of beer are, I believe, still
given to every person who knocks at the porter's lodge, the habit being a
remnant of the old days when charity and hospitality distinguished the
place.

We can understand how important this hospital and others like it were, when we remember how miserable the houses of the poor must have been; how dirt, salt diet, want of knowledge on many subjects, produced plagues, leprosy, and other bad diseases, so fearful, that good and rich people deemed it a privilege to found hospitals, where the sick and suffering could be cared for.

The entrance to the huge ancient kitchens and the "Hundred Men's Hall" is under a lofty tower, in which hangs the Curfew Bell, which every evening still sounds its warning that lights and fires are to be extinguished, proclaiming, even as it did when William the Norman ruled the land—

> "Darkness in chieftain's hall,
> Darkness in peasant's cot!"

Now let us pass from Hampshire, and through Wiltshire, where the great grey stones reared in the time of the Druids still remain; then on to the pleasant coast of Dorset and the Isle of Purbeck, where stand the remains of Corfe Castle, about which I want to tell you a story.

OLD ENGLISH DRINKING HORNS.

But wait and look across from Weymouth Bay to Portland. There is a great convict prison built on the top of those cliffs, and below them are about a hundred stone quarries, out of which all sorts of curious fossils are dug; even great stems of trees remain deep in the earth, all petrified and hardened into stone.

Notice the shingle or pebbly beaches along the south coast—round water-worn pebbles, which mostly are fragments of broken cliffs more or less washed by the tide. All this shingle has a slight eastward movement along the south coast of England, that is, from Cornwall onwards towards Kent. This is caused by the tides which flow in from the Atlantic driving the loose mass before them. Thus, the Solent, which divides the Isle of Wight from Hampshire, is crossed for more than two-thirds of its width by the shingle bank of Hurst Castle; while here is the Chesil Bank, a ridge of shingle almost ten miles long, and a quarter of a mile broad, which connects the Island of Portland to the mainland of Weymouth.

This Chesil Bank commences at Bridport, where it is merely sand ; this
becomes mixed up with pebbles, and these pebbles gradually become larger
and larger, till at Portland they are quite six inches across.   The inhabitants
say that if they lose their way on a dark night, they can tell exactly where
they are by feeling the size of these stones.   The shore is most dangerous in
stormy weather.   The bay on the west is called Deadman's Bay.   Once, when
a dreadful tempest was raging, the billows caught up a sloop that was tossing
among them, and heaving it upwards, landed it on the top of the bank, where
the astonished crew were able to get out and walk to Portland.   The vessel
was found high and dry, quite uninjured, and afterwards launched in the
Fleet, a narrow channel which separates the coast from the strange bank,
which had stood our mariners in such good stead.

WEYMOUTH PIER, AND THE ISLE OF PORTLAND.

HOW A BRAVE LADY DEFENDED HER CASTLE.

YOU all know something about the troubles in England during the days that King Charles and his Parliament were struggling for power; and it was about this time that my Lady Banks, wife of Chief Justice Banks, and her family retired to their domain, Corfe Castle, hoping for peace and quietness, and waiting for better times. But public affairs grew more and more disturbed; many battles were fought, and by the spring most of the king's castles had surrendered to the Parliamentary officers. Yet Corfe Castle, on the Isle of Purbeck, still held out for the king. That sturdy old fortress—the strongest in England, which, before the invention of artillery it would have been altogether hopeless to attack—was now to be taken, if possible, by treachery, if open force would not avail, that all the defences of the coast might be in the hands of the Roundheads, as the opponents of the king were commonly called, because of their short cropped hair.

One sunny May-day morning, the whole population of the little Isle of Purbeck was astir. There was blowing of horns, and merry shout and stir, such as there often used to be all over England in old May-days, when the king ruled the land; now it was different, for the grave Puritans loved not such light sounds, and holiday folks were looked upon with disgust. But here, about Corfe, it was an old usage, which even in those troubled times should not be set aside, that on this day the people had from ancient times permission from the lord of the castle to course a noble stag, with which he annually presented them, with great state of horns and hounds, and every one, rich or poor, always assembled on these occasions. But this time

more than were reckoned on came—even sturdy Parliamentary troopers on
horseback, to try to surprise and make prisoners the gentlemen hunting, and
to take the fortress from the Royalists.

My Lady Banks having heard of these
strangers, gave hasty orders to shut the
castle gates against all comers; and the
troopers, having missed their prey on the
hills, came riding in, a few at a time,
quietly asking if, this being free holiday,
they might be allowed to see over the fine
old place. They only wanted to admire it—
would do no mischief, they promised. "No,
certainly they might not enter," was the
stern and significant answer; even though
the commanders appeared quite shocked
that the lady should think, for one moment,
that they meant mischief. Not they; it was
curiosity—might they not beg for admission?

But still the answer was, "No;" no
strangers not in the king's service could enter
there; then away went the baffled troopers.
Soon came a message from the Commission
of the Houses of Parliament, that my lady
should give up the four small pieces of
cannon that were then in the castle, because
the people in the island complained that
these had been mounted, and that they were
afraid it meant mischief to them; but my
lady, though she offered to dismount the
pieces, just to satisfy the Commissioners,

NO ADMISSION!

refused to give them up, and preferred keeping them where they were for
her own protection, and to satisfy herself that no ill was intended.

All was quiet for a few days after that bold resolve, and the storm
appeared to have blown over. Early one morning, when all was still
within the castle walls, and no thought of danger and assault troubled
the few quiet sleepers—there were but five men and a few women—there

were heard sudden shouting and clamour at the gates, while the startled warder was summoned in hot haste to carry this message to his mistress, namely, that there were forty stout sailors come to demand the four pieces, in the name of the Parliamentary Commissioners at Poole; deny them who dare!

Dressing in haste, down came the brave lady to her gates, cool and unflinching, to demand of these fellows what their errand might be. She scorned the warrant they showed her, and bade them begone at once. Then, as they lingered, she called her small garrison, and setting them to work—the five men and the girls—mounted the contested pieces on their carriages again, and loading one, fired it with such effect that the sailors all went off as fast as they could go.

Then matters began to look serious; indeed, my lady understood that something must be done in earnest, and by beat of drum she gave the alarm to her tenants and friends in the neighbourhood, who came with what arms they could collect. But every day there also came threatening messages and letters, warning her that if she dared to collect arms, or to keep the four cannons on the ramparts, they, the Parliamentarians, would send armed forces for them. Also stern messages were sent to the homes of those who had come to her assistance, threatening that their houses should all be burned, and they themselves carried off to prison if they dared to help the rebellious lady.

And now pitiful scenes happened; for weeping wives and children came from the town to the castle, entreating the brave lady not to bring on them this ruin and misery—begging of their husbands and sons to return to their homes and protect their own families. Then, too, came a warning that some gunpowder that had been sent for by my lady had been discovered and stopped on its way, and that a proclamation had been made in the market-place that no beef, beer, or any other provisions should be sold to Lady Banks or her servants, on pain of imprisonment to all who sold, and that no messengers should, for the present, be allowed to pass in and out of the castle on any errand whatever. No wonder if at this time, being without ammunition or food to stand a siege, the lady's heart gave way—so far, at least, that she agreed to give up those four pieces, on condition that she should then be allowed to keep her castle in peace and quietness. The enemy promised all she liked, and took away the guns.

But the loyal lady doubted their promises and fair words ; and finding
that once they had carried off her cannon they grew careless of her doings,
she brought in a store of powder and provisions ; then hearing that some

PARLIAMENTARY SOLDIERS.

Royalist commanders were near, she sent them a secret message, begging
of them to remember how important a place Corfe was, and desiring them
to send her some one to take charge of the castle out of her weak hands, and
to keep it for the king. So they sent one Captain Laurence ; but he, not

having a proper royal commission, could not command money or provisions in time to be of service; for, as you may be sure, it was not long before the Parliament, hearing what was going on, sent troops to besiege the new power which had, through their own short-sightedness, risen in the strong old fortress by the sea.

Soon a force, between 200 or 300 horse and foot, and two pieces of ordnance, arrived, and having fired some houses in the town, summoned the castle to surrender; but finding that of no use, they departed, to be soon followed by over 500 men, who, early one misty morning, brought a large battle array, arms with quaint names, "a demi-cannon, a culverin, two sacres," and other weapons, with which they attacked the castle at every point. When these failed, they tried to bribe the besieged with promises of mercy and reward, or to frighten them into submission with threats of dire punishment, which, as you may fancy, were not even listened to.

And so for long, long hours and days the siege went wearily on. To make their approaches to the wall with more safety, they had brought two rough wooden engines, lined with wool to deaden the shot, called the "Sow" and the "Boar." The first that moved forward was the "Sow," but the musketeers of the castle aimed at her many legs, the only undefended part of her body, so that some of these ran away, and the rest fell to the ground quite useless; while the "Boar," seeing the ill success of his mate, would not even advance to the attack. Altogether, the assailants found it hard and troublesome work, even though they tore the lead off the church roof, and rolled it up and shot it at the garrison, never even stopping to cast it into musket-balls. And thus it went on for many days, when they seemed as far off from success as on the first day of the siege. But at last the Earl of Warwick having sent 150 mariners with cartloads of ammunition and scaling-ladders, the besiegers grew desperate; they resolved to make one grand effort to storm the castle on all sides. So they divided their forces into two parties: one to assault the middle ward, defended by Captain Laurence and the greater part of the soldiers, the other to attack the upper ward, which my brave Lady Banks, with her daughters, her women, and her five soldiers, undertook to keep with their lives.

Think what a strange, wild, heart-stirring scene it must have been! How difficult for us to realise in these peaceful days, when civil war is unknown, that mass of bold, angry, half-frantic men, armed to the teeth,

swarming up those scaling-ladders, swearing death and destruction to all
within those stone walls that had held them aloof so long, many of them
rude, rough men, heated and encouraged by promises of spoil, and prize and
plunder, and by threats of death and disgrace should they shrink from their
work or venture to return. But, above all, a stranger scene still, to see a
woman flying here and there, entreating, encouraging, promising, fighting,
while others, with set lips and pale faces, hold the ward in spite of powder
and balls, and armed men, with swords and daggers between their teeth.
They heave over great stones on the assailants; they fling down heavy
furniture on their heads; they cut the ropes as fast as the scaling-ladders
catch at any projecting point. It is for life and death and honour, for their
king, and for their fair, brave Lady Banks; never a weak girlish heart fails,
never a woman's hand shrinks; well do they hold their own; but still the foe
swarm, shouting and yelling, at their feet. How long can this last, how
long? There is a slight pause in all this turmoil; many a brave man lies
killed, and many another is wounded in the struggle, and still the old fortress
stands grim and grey in the falling shadows. Then there is heard a
distant murmur, as of far-off trampling feet, and men below hold their
breath to listen, and pale, haggard women above drop all unheeded the big
rough stones, and hot lead, and cruel war weapons they have boldly wielded,
to clasp their hands in thankfulness, and cry, on their knees, "Thank God, we
are saved; it is the Royalist army at last!"

And so, indeed, it was. Old Sir Watt Earl and Sydenham, who had
also heard the sound of many feet, hurried away from the battle-field, leaving
behind them a hundred men killed or hurt in this desperate siege, which had
lasted over six weeks, and which only cost the besieged two lives; and what was
more, the besiegers left their artillery and ammunition, which came in for
the use of the garrison and the king, whom my brave lady had so stead-
fastly defended. I believe that Corfe Castle still belongs to her descendants.
It is only a massive ruin now, but the grandest in the kingdom. In 1646 the
fortress was again besieged, or rather blockaded, by the Parliamentary forces;
but this time, instead of being defended by loyal hearts, it surrendered through
the treachery of an officer of the garrison. Then the Puritans, afraid, I suppose,
of attempting to keep such a powerful stronghold, ordered it to be demolished:
and so the walls and towers were undermined or blown up with gunpowder,
that they might never again be of use to shelter either king or subject.

QUEEN ELFRIDA'S TREACHERY.

THE LANDING OF MONMOUTH.

Here it was that wicked Queen Elfrida handed a cup of mead to her step-son Edward while she signed to an assassin to stab the luckless young king. Here too, in the days of that fierce, bad King John, it is said that a sad tragedy took place, for the king, having had some dispute with Sir William Brause, took him and his family prisoners, and held them fast in Corfe; but after a time he was persuaded to set Sir William at liberty, that he might try to raise a ransom of 60,000 marks. His prisoner, however, failing in the attempt, disguised himself as a beggar, and escaped to France, thinking, no doubt, that John, however enraged, would soon allow his wife and little boy to follow. But instead of that, the enraged monarch ordered that the fair Lady Maude and her son should be shut up in a room, with only a sheaf of corn and a small piece of raw bacon for food, that they might slowly starve, as a punishment for an offence which they had no hand in. There in that gloomy chamber they were left for eleven days, at the end of which the door was opened, and the two were found dead, but close clasped in each other's arms—sad victims of a time that allowed a cruel king such power over his innocent subjects.

The river Frome is the boundary of the Isle of Purbeck, which is very wild and rugged, with grand precipices and large caverns and chalk quarries. Near it there is a strange rock called the Dancing Ledge, on which the wild waves wash, and as they break they seem to dance and sparkle in the sun.

The most southern point of the island is St. Alban's Head, where a little chapel, built long ago for a priest to say masses in for the safety of passing sailors, has been changed into a coast-guard station, well furnished with ropes, and rockets, and boats, for the service of those in danger.

Before leaving Dorset let us visit Lyme Regis, where the pretty river Lyme flows through a deep valley into the sea. Here the unfortunate Duke of Monmouth landed, in 1685, on his ill-fated expedition to dethrone James the Second; and here he was met by hundreds of ploughmen with their scythes, and miners with rough weapons, who accompanied him to Taunton, where he assumed the title of king. A band of young maidens publicly presented him with a Bible and a gaily-embroidered flag; but his career ended on Tower Hill, and few of his unlucky followers returned to their poor homes in pleasant Dorsetshire.

ROUGH WEATHER OFF THE DEVONSHIRE COAST.

" 'Neath rustic roof, all flower clad,
He grew a bold and sturdy lad,
In pleasant Devon."

DEVONSHIRE.

LET us now visit fair, fruitful Devonshire, the third largest county in England. We shall see Dartmoor, all composed of granite, rising in great rocks or "Tors"—Yes Tor, Stag Tor, Sheep Tor, Fox Tor. The granite soil is covered with peat, where heather, moss, and ferns grow, while in the centre is a bog which would swallow us up if we were to tread on it. Beyond is Exmoor, where wild ponies and red deer still hide. But away from these moors Devon is as a fair green garden, a great apple orchard. Here and there are lovely lanes, picturesque little cottages hidden in sweet fuchsias, vines, and roses; and a clear, pure stream flows through almost every village.

I wish we had time to linger and think about all the clever people born in Devonshire: of Sir Francis Drake, Sir Walter Raleigh, Sir Humphrey Gilbert, who discovered Newfoundland; the painter, Sir Joshua Reynolds; the poets, Gay and Coleridge; and the famous Duke of Marlborough.

Let us linger at Teignmouth and Torbay, on which landed Prince William of Orange, when he came to seize the English crown. Here a quantity of fish is caught in trawling nets—large bags, twenty yards long,

ILFRACOMBE.

the mouths of which are kept open by wooden beams. They are trawled along the bottom of the bay, and soon filled with fish.

Yonder is Torquay, with its handsome houses. Sick people come from all parts to get health and strength from the pleasant sea breezes.

See, here is a sketch of Ilfracombe, a pretty, well-known town in North

Devon, on the south side of the Bristol Channel, and 200 miles from London. Its situation, and the irregularity of its steep and narrow streets, give the place a very singular appearance. It is built in a valley and along the side of a hill parallel with the sea. The principal street is almost a mile in length. The Capstone Parade, "a conical, flag-crowned mound of shale with veins of white quartz," is one of the finest marine promenades on the coast. Lantern Hill is approached from the quay, and the building on the top was once a chapel dedicated to the patron Saint of Fishermen, and now used as a light-house. This lighthouse is 100 feet above the sea. On the other side of the harbour mouth is the majestic Hillsborough, 500 feet high, commanding an extensive view of the coast and inland scenery. On the west of Capstone Hill are the Tors—consisting of seven shaggy peaks; and beyond is the frowning bluff of Bull Point. The whole aspect of the scenery is singularly grand and romantic; the beautiful bay and the glorious expanse of the Bristol Channel make a good many people want to linger there all the summer.

But here we are at Plymouth Sound, the most beautiful of all Devonshire bays. Three rivers fall into it—the Plym, the Laira, and the Tamar; and three large towns stand on it—Plymouth, Stonehouse, and Devonport.

The Sound is chiefly noted as a naval station, though it was a very dangerous one, because of the great Atlantic waves rolling inwards, until Mr. Rennie raised a stone rampart across their path. The citadel is strong, and well furnished with cannon. It is on the end of the Hoe, from whence we get a most beautiful view of land and water, cottages, and tall masts.

Let us wander up and down this grand walk, while I tell you the story of the Armada, for from this point it was first discovered advancing upon England.

"Attend, all ye who list to hear our noble England's praise;
I sing of the thrice famous deeds she wrought in ancient days,
When that great fleet invincible against her bore in vain
The richest spoils of Mexico, the stoutest hearts in Spain."

King Philip of Spain was one of the most powerful rulers in Europe, and a very bigoted member of the Roman Catholic Church. He was ever ready to do the utmost for his religion, and he waged war with many Protestant countries, persecuting their inhabitants in a manner terrible to think of. He determined to make a conquest of England, which was then the foremost of the Reformed nations of Europe, and whose queen, Elizabeth, was strongly opposed to his policy. If he succeeded in making a Spanish province of England, he would not only strengthen his European power, but would also provide more security for his vast West Indian possessions, which were being continually attacked by the daring enterprise of the many brave sailors who flourished during "Good Queen Bess's" long reign.

So King Philip, having thought the matter well over, went to work in right royal earnest. He got together arms from Genoa and Venice, and a great supply of money and troops from all parts of his own dominions, and made preparations of the greatest magnitude to carry out his ideas, both by sea and land; especially by sea, because, England being an island, it was only by sea that he could visit her.

There was a great though gradual stir in England, when every day fresh accounts came of the terrible armament preparing in Spain. The queen, though brave-hearted, was fully aware of the danger of a conflict with the mighty power of Spain, and she did her best to pacify King Philip, and persuade him to stop at home. But her brave captains at sea, who knew by experience what kind of enemy they had to deal with, and did not believe in his giving up so grand and promising a scheme, soon begged that no more time might be wasted in writing and talking. So, after a great deal of preparation, the famous Sir Francis Drake was at last sent off with thirty ships, and away he sailed to the Spanish harbour of Cadiz, and destroyed or captured thirty of the enemy's ships, by way of beginning business; or, as he termed it, "Singeing ye Kinge of Spaine's bearde."

Next he took a turn round the coast, and disposed of about a hundred more vessels of one sort or another, besides demolishing three or four castles. Then he returned to the Tagus, and captured the *Santa Phillipe*, a very large ship, loaded with merchandise, while he challenged the Marquis of Santa Cruz, the best sea captain in Spain, to come out and meet him. But Philip, the king, who was not quite ready, would not allow him to do so; and some say that the poor brave marquis was so mortified at this that he died of vexation and disappointment.

On finding that, though little was said, mighty preparations for an invasion of England were going on all this time, Queen Elizabeth called a council of war, and it was decided to face the enemy before they set foot on our land. It was thought possible that the Spaniards might attempt to sail up the Thames as far as Gravesend, perhaps. Both sides of the river were fortified, and a great camp assembled at Tilbury Fort, where a bridge of ships was formed across the river. There came great numbers of militia

THE BRITISH FLEET OFF CADIZ.

and volunteers from all parts; and then, with much state and pomp, came Elizabeth, "the woman" who ruled England, and whom Philip intended to dethrone. She came partly dressed in armour, riding on a strong war-horse, carrying her head erect, and in her hand "ye truncheone or staffe of a common capitaine," and looking firmly round her, she made this speech to her loyal subjects assembled :—

"I am come amongst you at this time, not for my own recreation or sport, but being resolved, in the midst and heat of battle to live and die amongst you all; and I would have you know, mine own good people, that though I have but the body of a weak feeble woman, I have the heart of a king, and of a king of England! and think it full scorn that Parma, or Spain, or any province of Europe should dare to invade my realm!" And so she talked bravely for a long time, and her own good people cheered loudly.

Tilbury Fort was very different from what it is now, with its great stone gateway, which was erected soon after this panic. The bastions are said to be the largest in England, the ramparts are mounted with heavy guns, and the whole of the level round it can be laid under water, if required.

Our English navy was not particularly flourishing at this time—long before the days of steam, remember. We had only about thirty sail; but in view of this common peril, nobles and private persons fitted out ships at their own expense, while our honest allies, the Dutch, who feared and hated the Spaniards, came forward to help with sixty ships and many promises; and Drake, Hawkins, Frobisher, and Seymour were appointed, under Lord Howard of Effingham, to command the sea forces—all being tried men and true.

It was on a Friday, the 29th of June, 1588, that the mighty Spanish fleet rode at last into English waters off Lizard Point, while more than twice five thousand beacon-fires blazed over English ground—tongues of fire, telling the news from Cornwall to Kent, and from Hampshire to Cumberland Macaulay paints the scene for us :—

> "It was about the lovely close of a warm summer's day,
> There came a gallant merchant ship full sail to Plymouth Bay;
> The crew had seen Castile's black fleet, beyond Aurigny's isle,
> At earliest twilight, on the waves, lie heaving many a mile.
> At sunrise she escaped their van, by God's especial grace;
> And the tall Pinta, till the noon, had held her close in chase.
> Forthwith a guard at every gun was placed along the wall;
> The beacon blazed upon the roof of Edgecombe's lofty hall;
> Many a light fishing-bark put out, to pry along the coast:
> And with loose rein and bloody spur rode inland many a post.
> From Eddystone to Berwick bounds, from Lynn to Milford Bay,
> That time of slumber was as bright, as busy, as the day;
> For swift to east, and swift to west, the warning radiance spread—
> High on St. Michael's Mount it shone—it shone on Beachy Head.

QUEEN ELIZABETH AT TILBURY.

Far o'er the deep, the Spaniard saw, along each southern shire,
Cape beyond cape, in endless range, those twinkling points of fire.
The sentinel on Whitehall Gate looked forth into the night,
And saw, o'erhanging Richmond Hill, that streak of blood-red light.
The bugle's note and cannon's roar the deathlike silence broke,
And with one bound, and with one cry, the royal city woke."

And oh! what a thrill must have run through our land when the first tidings were brought of the undoubted approach of the great Invincible Armada, that was coming proudly to conquer and destroy the independence, faith, and liberty of the little island, whose people had for long enough been a thorn in the sides of the Spaniards' pride and prosperity.

For five years this terrible avenging fleet had been preparing, and now it was coming fast over the seas—so cried Fleming, the Scottish privateer. He had caught sight of it over the Lizards, and had a narrow escape of being taken prisoner. He was the first to bring the news to Vice-Admiral Blake and his officers, who at that moment were playing bowls on the Plymouth Hoe. There was a sudden bustle and rush and call for ships and boats —all was stir and excitement. But the admiral stood calm and unmoved amidst it all, insisting on finishing the game. "There was plenty of time," he said, coolly, "to win the game and beat the Spaniards!" Yet all this time that terrible fleet was approaching our coast, forming a crescent seven miles broad—think of that, boys!—composed of ninety-two ships of the line, thirty frigates, thirty transports for horses, and four galleys. Remember, that in those days our coast was not defended as it is now; the royal navy was small; there was no standing army—all our best troops were absent in Flanders; and no foreign country was able or willing to assist us; indeed, poor England seemed in a hopeless case.

What a sight those splendid Spanish ships were, built up like castles, covered with awnings and gilding, with their crews all flushed and expectant; and the bands playing merry music on deck. How insignificant our little vessels must have looked to their captain, General Medina Sidonia, as he, with the vicar of the Holy Inquisition and others of the proudest nobles of Castile by his side, stood in his own "private shot-proof fortress," and surveyed the enemy. Presently the Spanish tried to get the English to begin a general engagement; but the latter knew better, only darting here, and there, and everywhere, doing what damage they could, without getting hurt themselves.

Soon some of the Spanish galleys were destroyed, others were harassed and injured, and the admiral was so disgusted with the seamanship of his captains, that he sent an officer on board of each ship with written sailing directions, and a hangman, with orders to hang, without delay, any captain who refused to obey them at once ; while another messenger went hurrying off in a sloop to inquire when the Duke of Parma was going to make his appearance on the scene; for I forgot to mention that the duke, with 30,000 men, had been ordered to embark in a number of flat-bottomed boats prepared for the occasion, and to join the Armada. As soon as the great fleet had overcome such opposition as might be offered, it was to land at Dover, proceed at once to London, and straightway capture that town. Sidonia was to go and seize upon the Isle of Wight, and fortify it, making all things convenient before proceeding to conquer Ireland. Now, all this was very simple and effective, only as the Duke of Parma, his 30,000 men, and his flat-bottomed boats happened to be all blockaded in the Flemish ports, where they could not possibly get out or help themselves, that part of King Philip's plan fell through, and the admiral was very much astonished and disappointed to find he had the whole difficult task to himself. And it was a difficult task; for though the English forces were not to be compared in numbers to those of the approaching enemy, they were led by brave, true hearts that knew no fear. Sir Walter Raleigh took the command of our land forces, and the heroic Drake, having leisurely finished his game of bowls, did wonders when the issue came; indeed, it was by the squadron he commanded that the principal execution was done upon the Armada, as it struggled in confusion against the valour of the English and the fury of the tempestuous seas. One enormous Spanish vessel surrendered without firing a shot, from very terror of the name of Drake, while other "Invincibles" were crippled and conquered by this dread commander, who, having found a hoard of 55,000 ducats on one of them, instantly shared them among his men, reserving no part for himself, in the open-hearted fashion of the times.

To the Spaniards, in their great war castles, our small vessels must have appeared like toy-ships tossing upon the waves. But they were toys destined to work them mischief, for they danced in and about those huge Spanish vessels, pouring fire and flame upon them in every direction. Then, in the dead of the night, came floating terrible fire-ships, piled high with sulphur, rosin, pitch—all sorts of dreadful things that burned fierce and terrible, breaking the firm line of that proud Spanish array; and during the night, the ships, trying to escape in the darkness, ran against each other, were burnt, sunk,

or destroyed; others drifted far out alone and unprotected on the wide sea, where the storm and wild tempest fought for England, and finished the work. The "Invincible" Armada was but a broken and shattered wreck. The coasts of Norway, Scotland, and Ireland were strewn with its wrecks. Out of the hundred and thirty-four vessels which sailed so triumphantly out of Corunna in July, only fifty-three, damaged and worthless, reached Spain again; and out of 30,000 men only 10,000 returned. So general was the mourning worn, that the king, looking upon it, no doubt, as a mute reproach, issued an edict forbidding his subjects to wear it; and when one unlucky man made a joke about "the Invincible," he was hanged by Philip's orders.

Do you wonder how his majesty felt when the news of the dreadful defeat reached him? You must guess at that, for in those days Spanish monarchs were taught to hide their vexation. He was writing a letter, and when the

A FIRE-SHIP AT WORK.

breathless messenger had told his terrible tale, Philip merely remarked that "he thanked God that he could fit out another such an expedition if he chose to do so," and continued his letter-writing as though nothing was the matter. I need scarcely mention, children, that he did not "choose."

WRECK OF ONE OF THE VESSELS OF THE ARMADA OFF THE IRISH COAST.

With what a stir of thankfulness and rejoicing every free-born Englishman's heart must have beat when the news rang through the land that the enemy, so long expected and dreaded by many, had gone their way back, defeated and baffled, to their own country.   How fast the tidings must have been carried from town to town—"post-haste"—there was no penny post then ; men had to ride with public news from one place to another, and proclaim them at the market-places.   And now, when it came to "the royal city," Queen Bess, dressed this time not in warlike but in gorgeous array, and followed by a long train of courtiers, statesmen, and fair and noble dames, came through the city streets, smiling at the happy faces of her joyful subjects.   Then when she reached the cathedral of St. Paul's, the lion-hearted queen knelt humbly at the west door, and publicly thanked God, who had thus delivered her land from the rage of the enemy.

But let me copy what an old writer tells us in his quaint fashion, as it will give you a capital idea of the scene of rejoicing on that 29th of November.

" Likewise, the Queen's majestic herself, imitating the ancient Romans, rode into London in triumph, in regard of her own and her subjects' glorious deliverance, for being attended upon very solemnly by all the principal estates and officers of her realm, she was carried through her said city of London in a triumphal chariot and in robes of triumph, from her palace into the said cathedral church of St. Paul's, out of which the ensigns and colours of the vanquished Spaniards hung displayed ; and all the citizens of London in their liveries stood on either side of the street by their several companies, with their ensigns and banners ; and the streets were hanged on both sides with blue cloth, which, together with the foresaid banners, yielded a very stately and gallant prospect.   Her majestie being entered into the church, together with the clergy and nobles, gave thanks unto God, and caused a public sermon to be preached before her, at Paul's Cross, wherever none other argument was handled, but that praise, honour, and glory might be rendered unto God, and that God's name might be extolled by thanksgiving ; and with her own princely voice she most Christianly exhorted the people to do the same, whereunto the people, with a loud acclamation, wished her a long and happy life, to the confusion of her foes."

Medals were struck, on which were the words, "It came, It saw, It fled;" and so it happened.   It fled away, like a herd of frightened deer, away northwards, past the Orkneys and Shetlands, catching up a few stray fisher-men as guides about the strange, wild coasts ; past the coast of Norway, and on, on, until weary, shattered, and dispirited, the few returned to tell the tale of disgrace, defeat, and loss, most totally unexpected by their confident friends at home.

No wonder that about this time Shakespeare wrote—

> " This England never did and never shall
> Lie at the proud feet of a conqueror ; "

or that the people sang—

> " Oh, where be those gay Spaniards,
> Which make so great a boast, O ?
> Oh, they shall eat the grey goose feather,
> And we shall eat the roast, O ! "

Excepting on the moors, Devonshire is, as I have told you, very fertile, especially the Vale of Exeter and the South Hams, that part between Dart-moor and the Channel, which is well called the " Garden of Devon." There grow in great abundance the pretty but bitter little apples, which are carried in cart-loads to the pound-houses to be crushed and squeezed, and finally bottled, and sent to all parts of England. Who has not heard of cider, clotted cream, and junket and cream cheese—all Devonshire dainties ? The county is also rich below its pleasant surface, hiding a great deal of fine potters' clay, valuable freestone and granite, tin, copper, and lead ; and as the climate is very pleasant, we might linger in the green lanes a very long time, had we only leisure.

The shore westward forms a curve, called Start Bay ; the cliffs here are formed of slate and gneiss, which sometimes looks very peculiar. This bay ends in Start Point, where stands a lighthouse, whose revolving light is almost the last sign our Indian or Australian outward-bound travellers see of England.

A CORNISH FISHING VILLAGE AFTER THE DAY'S WORK.

THE CORNISH COAST.

CORNWALL.

"By Pol and Pen
You may know the Cornish men."

WE cannot go "roundabout" and miss Cornwall, the birth-place of famous "King Arthur of the Round Table," with its wild and beautiful sea coast, where the Atlantic dashes in such fury that nothing but the hardest kinds of rocks remain to greet it—granite, slate, and the pretty greenish serpentine. Inland, on the wild moors, huge masses of granite are piled, some flung there by Nature, some reared by those priests and lawgivers of our forefathers, the Druids, who, as we have read in the ancient story of our land, loved to perform the services of their wild gods on these natural altars, which even Time's strong hand has been unable to destroy.

Cornwall is a very rich county, though you might scarcely think so, to look at its stony surface. But its riches are hidden deep under-ground, like those of the gnomes and elves of fairy tales; lead, tin, and copper

BIRTHPLACE OF SIR HUMPHRY DAVY, PENZANCE.

lie heaped far from the light of day. We all know how the business-like Phœnicians once upon a time traded with the Britons for tin. Near Penzance is the village of Marazion, where the Jews once held tin-markets; they called it Mare-zion, or Bitter-zion. The copper mines were not discovered until some two hundred years ago. At first, the ignorant miners called it "dust," and when they found it, often gave up their working in disgust, declaring that the tin was spoilt by this tiresome stuff. They soon learned its value, however, and now I am told that over 30,000 miners are employed in Cornwall and Devonshire.

But let us begin by paying a visit to Penzance, where we shall see the house in which the great Sir Humphry Davy was born. You will remember that it was he who invented the safety lamp, which enables the workers in coal-mines to carry a light without fear of setting fire to the "fire-damp," or gas, which collects in the mines. Speaking about gas reminds me of a curious idea which the people here have, that is, that the air in the copper-mines prevents decomposition, and will preserve unchanged any dead body; in proof of which they tell a touching story. It is of a miner who was missed the day before his wedding. He was searched for far and near, but in vain. The poor young bride was almost broken-hearted; his old parents died of grief at his loss; his brothers, and sisters, and friends missed and mourned for him. But years passed on, and they grew old, and one by one died away. The story was forgotten by all, except the faithful girl he had loved—not young now, but faded, bent, and grey, a very old, old woman. Full sixty years had passed, and the little village, hidden in the Cornish hills, was all quiet and unchanged, the busy miners came and went to their work deep in the molten earth; and women spun, cooked, and scolded, or helped to wash the ore their husbands had dug up; there was little stir and life. But one hot summer's afternoon, on opening some old forgotten shaft, that must have long since fallen in unheeded, the body of a fair youth was found—a miner, by his dress, yet a stranger to all present. And many old and young came to look, and wonder who could it be? But I had better end the story in the touching words of one better skilled than I am to tell it :—

"They brought him from the dusky mine,
  With kind but fruitless care ;
Yet few at first could hope resign,
  He lay so calm and fair.

"Strange, that beneath a mass of earth,
  So heavy and so deep,
The youth should thus be lifted forth,
  Like living man asleep.

"None knew the face, yet it was fair,
  Not twenty summers old ;

Around the snowy brow the hair
  Fell thick, in curls of gold.

"That earth, from taint of all decay,
  Mortality can screen ;
And who can guess how many a day
  The body there had been ?

"The crowding miners gathered round ;
  Their garb the stripling wore,
But of them all could none be found
  Had seen that face before.

"Soon every village wife and maid
  Arrived, the tumult pressed ;
Each trembled lest the comely dead
  Were him she loved the best.

"His was no form to be passed by,
  No face to be forgot ;
Yet of that thronging company,
  All owned they knew him not.

"The spirits of the mine with ease
  Can varying shapes assume ;
This form may harbour one of these—
  No tenant of the tomb.

"All scattered back, a shapeless dread
  Turned every heart to stone.

'Mid a wide circle lay the dead,
  In beauty, all alone ;

"When, peering through the fearful crowd,
  A wrinkled woman old
Crept slowly forth, and screamed aloud,
  That visage to behold.

"She was his love ; oh ! contrast strange
  In years. in form, in limb ;
Life hath on her wrought drearier change
  Than death hath brought to him.

"The pitying crowd was moved to ruth,
  All felt the sight appalling ;
The bitter, burning tears of youth
  From such old eyelids falling."

And now let me show you the tall chimney of a copper-mine. It belongs to the immense steam-engine that pumps the water out. In one place the pumping-rod is the third of a mile long, and sometimes pumps up 1,600 gallons in a minute. If this water were left below it would destroy the miners ; but being raised, it serves to cleanse the copper ore.

See, there is the deep shaft that leads to the bottom of the pit. It is divided into two parts—one for bringing up ore, the other for the miners. If any one would like to descend with them, he will have to change his dress, and put on a suit of coarse flannel, a kind of night-cap, and a big hard round hat, to the brim of which a tallow candle will be stuck by means of a lump of wet clay ; then he may go down, down, down—a dreary journey, I can promise. From the shaft different galleries branch off and run underground in every direction, and in these hot, dim galleries, or passages, we find the poor miners at work, sometimes in little parties of three or four, sometimes alone. In the lower passages it gets duller and hotter, and the poor fellows can scarcely bear any clothes on them. When a light is held against its rough walls they look very beautiful, sometimes bright shining green, with red streaks in it ; that is the metal itself.

Sometimes these galleries extend under the sea, and then the miners hear a dull, distant moaning as they work—a sad, low, unearthly sound, ever repeating itself—that is, when the waves are still above their heads. But when a tempest comes on, then the sounds change, and become so terrible that even the miners tremble and shudder, for it seems as though the mad waters must break in and wash them all away.

West of Penzance a mine was actually sunk in the sea, a kind of chimney rising from the shaft; but this is an exception. How glad the poor fellows must be when their day's work of eight long hours is over—when they once more see the blue skies, breathe fresh air, wash, put on decent clothes, and go home to their humble cottages, where, let us hope, kind wives and bright-eyed children are waiting to greet dear father.

INTERIOR OF A COPPER-MINE.

Old Cornish folks had many quaint customs, some of which are still practised—such as the lighting of tar-barrels on the eves of St. John and St. Peter. From these principal lights boys and girls light torches, and run hard through the streets, whirling their flaming brands, and shouting, "An eye! an eye! an eye!" Then they suddenly stop, and the first two raise their arms, forming an eye, as they call it, through which the long string of laughing followers pass—just what you children call "Threading the Needle" in the old country dances at Christmas time.

One place which has its story is Tintagel Castle, in the north of Cornwall. It is a fine old ruin, perched on the summit of grand piled-up rocks that jut out into the sea; the cliffs are formed of slate. It is sometimes called King Arthur's Castle, for here it is said that the famous king was born, and here, too, he died, in 542—at least, so tradition says :—

> " The bravest of all knights was he,
>   And bore himself right manfully :
>   Towards lofty ones he aye was stour,
>   But meek and piteous to the poor.

> " Arthur, saith the history,
>   In the heart was stricken mortally ;
>   And thence to Avalon was borne,
>   That healed his wounds might be.
>   The prophet Merlin told—
>   He said that Arthur's end should be
>   For aye enwrapped in mystery ;
>   And truly said, that still his fame
>   Should last, and foemen dread his name."

He left the fortress in an early morning to encounter his rebellious nephew, Modred, but at night his downcast followers returned, bearing their beloved chief's body, slain by Modred's own hand. The place where he was killed is still pointed out near Camelford ; they call it Slaughter Bridge to this day. It must have been a desperate encounter indeed, for we are told that for ages after piles of armour, rings, and brass furniture for horses were still dug up hereabouts. To use an old historian's words, " Upon the river Camel, neare to Camelforde, was the last dismal battel strocken between the noble King Arthur and his treacherous nephew, Modred, where the one took his death, and the other his death wound."

In old days the coast towns of Cornwall often had uneasy times of it, for here the enemies' ships would land, and burn the houses, and slay all who tried to stop them. For instance, in 1595, when the Spaniards had began to recover from the defeat of their great Armada, a body of these revengeful warlike folk suddenly landed and burned Penzance, and the pretty, peaceful villages of Newlyn and Mousehole, and even St. Paul's Church, which stood alone in the fields, scarcely any resistance being made, as the simple, superstitious inhabitants suddenly remembered some old prediction, informing them that—

> " Strangers would land
>   On the rocks on Merlin.
>   To burn Paul's church,
>   Penzance, and Newlyn.'

And so they let them do it—I should think somewhat to the surprise of the warlike Spaniards, who were not used to such easy victories; and having done all the mischief they could, re-assembled on the beach, embarked, and sailed quietly away.

About the coast of Cornwall the Pilchard, sometimes called the Gipsy

THE SPANIARDS' VISIT TO PENZANCE.

Herring, causes much excitement. Men called "huers" watch day and night on the highest cliffs, about the month of October, to be ready to signal the boats the moment they see indications of an approaching shoal; for, like the herring, these fish traverse the seas in great columns, though where they all come from no one exactly knows; but on comes the shoal like the shadow of a great cloud on the sea, and as it approaches the shore, thousands of pretty silvery little fish may be seen jumping joyously in and out of the troubled waters. Then the "huer" gives his signal, the boat is manned, and flies out into the bay, bearing with it a great net, or "seine," having a very small mesh, and costing, perhaps, £150. It is 500 or 600 yards long. All the "shooters" who man the boat keep their eyes upon the "huer," who stands with a bush in his hand, by which he guides the boat. As soon as the shoal is well in the bay he gives a signal, and steadily and carefully the men pay out the long net; the lower side being weighted with lead, rapidly sinks, while a line of cork-floats keeps the edge of the other

PILCHARD.

side on the surface. Slowly and silently the "seine" is cast outside the shoal, then the ends of the net are gradually pulled near the shore and made fast—and so are all the shining, silvery pilchards, for never again will they visit their native seas.

For now watch, here comes another boat, and that one casts a second net, called a "tuck," inside the big one called "seine;" this is to stir up the fish and bring them to the surface, and then suddenly, with a mighty shout, there comes a great rush of boats and barges, crowded with excited fisher-people. The shore, too, is lined with a lively, noisy crowd, men shouting, dogs barking, women calling, children laughing: but above all we hear the loud, steady "Yo! heave ho!" of the haulers, which continues until the shoal is borne upon the surface — a sight for the fishermen to gratefully rejoice at, as they dip out the silvery, struggling captives in baskets and buckets, and empty them from the net into the boats, which are soon filled to overflowing: then away they go, to return soon for another dip, until the whole shoal is captured and carried off to market.

Wandering about this part of England, we cannot miss one celebrated place near the Land's End, Cornwall. There stands the "Logan Stone," a huge block of granite, balancing itself in such an odd way that the least touch is enough to set it rocking or "tossing," and it looks as though fall it must, though all the strength of many men would not tumble it over from the pile of rocks on which it is perched.

The simple country people used to declare that nothing could displace this wonderful rocking-stone. But one day, a young lieutenant, having

THE LOGAN STONE, CORNWALL.

nothing better to do, determined to try what the strength of a party of English sailors could accomplish; so they pushed and pulled with such vigour that at length the big stone, to the loud wonder and delight of the mischievous sailors, reeled and shook, and finally toppled over, much to the disgust of the dwellers thereabouts, who made such an outcry to the authorities that our clever, idle fellows were ordered to get the "Logan Stone" into its old place again. And a far more difficult task it proved than the getting it down; they had to fetch ropes and tackle from Plymouth, and it took twice the trouble to hoist the huge rock on its old perch; but they did it at last, and there it rocks to this very day, just as you see in the picture; and there, judging from appearances, it will remain for ages to come.

On these wild moors many huge masses of granite are piled, some by the hand of Nature, others by the Druids of old, those priests whose religion taught them to worship the Supreme Power amidst forests, waters, and rocks, and whose altars, stone pillars, and cromlechs still remain scattered about in many countries. We have a great number in England. Perhaps some of you will have seen the *Cor-gawr*, or Dance of Giants, Stonehenge, the remains of a sacred circle, or "cromlech," supposed to have been once used as a kind of temple or assembly hall. Dolmenstones placed one on another were usually tombs, not temples; one of the largest known is in Cornwall, it is a kind of table placed on two rocks. About a group called the Hurlers, some will tell

NATURAL GRANITE ROCKS.

you that they were a party of men who were playing at ball, or "hurling," on Sunday, and punished by being turned into stone as they stood ; but others say that they are simply the remains of a Druidical temple, and I must say I think the latter statement is the more correct.

When I was a child there was a funny old custom at Looe, in south-east Cornwall, where the folks turned out early on May morning to pluck a sprig of the narrow-leaved elm ; this leaf, called "May," was to be worn all the day. As soon as this "May" was secured and breakfast hurried through, all the boys assembled on the banks of the stream, or "gutter," that usually flows through a Cornish town, each boy carrying a dipping-horn, that is, a bullock's horn with the point sawn off, fixed at the end of a stout stick ; this was intended to carry water with which to drench folks. But as it was considered only right to ask the mayor's permission for what followed, the boldest boys proceeded to that gentleman's house, and his worship knowing well enough what they wanted, came to the door, and asked, good-naturedly, "Well, boys, what is it ? "

"Please, sir, may we dip ? "

"Certainly! any one without 'May ;' but mind you don't dip any one else, or you'll get into trouble."

"Yes, sir." And so, the permission obtained, as it had been from time immemorial, the merry crew walked off and watched for their opportunity to dip forgetful people ; few of the inhabitants could be met with without the May-day sprig, but as soon as any stranger appeared without the green badge, the crowd would surround them, crying, "Ha'penny, a penny, or a good wet back!" and if the coin were not handed to them at once, the unlucky victim was drenched without delay or mercy, and then would scamper off as fast as he could.

This dipping was to the boys great fun. As night came on, workmen and others joined in the frolic, hiding behind walls or corners with pails full of water, which they would empty out on any rash passer-by, even though, holding out the leaves, he should shout, "I say, stop, here is my May!" The laughing answer would be, "Dip after sunset, May or no May!" But this custom has almost died out in these days, I believe, though it was a common one when I was a boy, with a dipping-horn of my own.

MONMOUTH.

AND now let us turn to a very old county, bordering on Wales; indeed, it was once part of Wales, and many Welsh customs and manners still linger there.

I think there are few counties in England where more grand old ruins are to be pointed out, owing to the fact that, in Norman times, it was mostly held and defended by nobles, called Lord Marchers. These feudal lords built more than twenty castles, the ruins of which still remain.

The ruins of the Castle of Monmouth owe much of their interest, in our eyes, to the fact that it was the birthplace of our famous King Henry V., "Harry of Monmouth." We are shown his cradle in an upper story of the ruins; it is an oblong wooden chest, swinging by links of iron between two standards, over which peer two birds, but I believe this is really the cradle of Edward II., and that the right one is to be seen at Troy House, half a mile out of the town, together with the armour which Henry wore at the Battle of Agincourt.

CRADLE OF HENRY V.

See, too, there is St. Mary's Church, the remains of a Benedictine priory; and there we may see the study of Geoffrey of Monmouth, a famous historian.

Chepstow is a busy little place, nestled among green trees, and its pride is the remains of Chepstow Castle, overhanging the pretty river Wye—so full of rapids and weirs, which we can cross in a large barge with sails, called a "trow." I wish I had space for half the stories connected with the grim old fortress, beginning with that of Roger de Britolior, a Norman lord, who chose to offend the Conqueror, and was put in prison forthwith; however, it seems that at the Easter festival the king's heart relented, and he sent his troublesome vassal a present of his own royal robes—an odd thing it seems to us, though in those days considered as a great mark of favour—but Roger did not appreciate

MONMOUTH CASTLE AND ST. MARY'S CHURCH.

it, for we are told that he so disdained the favour that he forthwith caused
a great fire to be made, and the mantle, the inner surcoat of silk, and the fair
upper garment lined with precious furs to be suddenly burnt, which being
told to the king, he swore a solemn oath that this disloyal Roger should never
again leave prison; and so his temper cost him liberty and fair Chepstow
Castle—rather a heavy price to pay for its indulgence.

At the time of the civil war the fortress was held by a small but gallant band of Royalists; and though Cromwell brought great forces against it, it seemed all in vain—the garrison defended themselves until all provisions were gone; and even then refused to surrender, unless under promise of quarter, thinking, if this were refused, they would attempt to escape by means of a boat, all ready for the purpose; but one of Cromwell's "Ironsides" swam across the Wye, with a knife held fast between his teeth, cut the cable, and drew it away beyond their reach. The fortress was again attacked, and most of its brave defenders slain.

Between Monmouth and Chepstow stand the remains of Tintern Abbey—one of the finest ruins in England. It was founded more than seven hundred years ago; now only some of the arches and stone walls remain, half hidden in ivy and creeping plants.

The Usk, another fine river, into which flows the Gavenny, brings us to the town of Abergavenny, which was once famous for the manufacture of gentlemen's perriwigs, made from the lovely white hair of the goats which wander free among the mountains hereabouts. Now it is noted for its blankets, and the encouragement it gives to all that is Welsh—music, history, or manufactures. Further down the Usk is Caerleon, once the capital of Wales, and long years ago reckoned the third largest town in Great Britain. There King Arthur held his Court, and called his friends to join him at his Table Round. But all this is as a dream of the past. Caerleon is a silent little place, and Newport, five miles from the mouth of the Usk, is the largest town in Monmouthshire.

RECEPTION OF QUEEN ELIZABETH AT KENILWORTH.

RUINS OF KENILWORTH CASTLE.

KENILWORTH.

MOST of you will know Kenilworth, by name, at least, for here the celebrated
Queen Elizabeth came to visit the great Dudley, Earl of Leicester. She rode
all the way from London on horseback—there were no railways then—and
was entertained by her loyal subject for seventeen days, at a cost of a
thousand pounds a day—a very large sum indeed in those times; but

> " No feats of prowess, joust, or tilt
> Of harness'd knights, or rustic revelry
> Were wanting"

F.

at this right loyal reception. Perhaps you may wonder how so much money could be spent in feasting; but you must remember that the queen brought her ladies and thirty-one barons in her train, and that it took over four hundred servants to wait on them. This will give you some idea of the size and style of the grand old fortress where room was found for so many. As to food, it is on record, that, besides all the rest, ten oxen were killed every morning, and sixteen hogsheads of wine were drank each day by this thirsty crowd; truly, a visit from her majesty was an expensive honour. But would you like to know the way the queen was served in those days, when it was well understood that she liked show and "braverie?" Let us listen to an eye-witness of the scene, only he must speak more modern English, or you will not understand him :—"On her entrance into the tilt-yard, a porter, tall and stern, wrapped in silk, with a huge club and a number of keys, came out to ask, as though in a great passion, but in metre made for the purpose, the cause of all this din and noise and riding about the place; but on seeing the queen, he fell straight down on his knees, begged her pardon, gave up his club and keys, and proclaimed free passage to all comers. Then came six trumpeters, clad in long garments of silk, sounding a tune of welcome on silvery trumpets five feet long, these harmonious 'blasters,'" as our witness calls them, "keeping up their music while the queen rode along the tilt-yard into the inner gate, where she was surprised by the sight of a floating island on a large pool, and on it a lovely lady of the lake and many maidens, surrounded by blazing torches; the lady made fine speeches in metre, which pageant was closed with a burst of music."

Then came another pretty sight—for, riding over a fair bridge erected for the purpose, that she might cross no common road, her majesty was presented with offerings by persons dressed to represent the heathen gods and goddesses: Sylvanus, god of the woods, gave her live bitterns, curlews, and other such dainty birds; Pomona presented her with apples, pears, and lemons; while Ceres laid before her ears of corn; and Bacchus, god of wine, huge clusters of grapes, both red and white. Truly, it must have been a pretty sight! And others followed, until at last the queen descended from her palfrey, and went wearied to her chamber, which was the signal for a loud sound of guns and "fyr-works." After that, every day and all day, all kinds of diversions followed for the amusement of the queen and her court, some of them sounding very odd to our ears—tilts, tournaments, deer-hunting, bear and bull-baiting—that cruel sport had not gone out of date; indeed, it was much enjoyed by her majesty, untroubled as she was by fine feelings—tumblers, rope-dancing, prize-fighting, morris-dancing, running at the quintain, and more "fyr-works."

RUNNING AT THE QUINTAIN.

And all the time there was feasting of the richest kind going on everywhere, and a great banquet every day at two o'clock—people kept early hours then— so that the old castle rang with music, mirth, and revelry from morning till night; while from all the country round trooped sight-seers, to look on and wonder. Are you tired of hearing of it all? or would you like to know that the old Coventry play of "Hock Tuesday" was performed before the queen, by certain good-hearted men of Coventry, who made her majesty laugh by the way in which they represented the insolence of the Danes, the corrupt act of Huna, King Ethelred's chieftain—his plot to destroy these invaders— the violent encounter between the Danish and English knights on horse-

STRATFORD-ON-AVON CHURCH.

back, all armed with spear and shield, which terrible fray was ended by the English women, who took the Danes captive, much to every one's delight ?

To show the hospitality of the noble host, "the clok bell sank not a note all the while her highness was thear," always pointing to two o'clock, the hour of the banquet. Another odd sight to entertain a queen with was the rude imitation of a country bridal—the bride, the groom, and bridesmaids all as ugly and oddly dressed as could be ; but it served the purpose well, for the queen laughed, and so I suppose the Earl of Leicester was satisfied that his most royal and capricious visitor was pleased with the entertainment.

Near to Kenilworth, which is in Warwickshire, and about as far from the
sea as it well can be, are many places you have all heard about.   Warwick
Castle, where lived the great Earls of Warwick, of one of whom—Guy of
Warwick—a strange story is told—how, when the Danes were advancing into

SHAKESPEARE'S BIRTH-PLACE.

England to dethrone the Saxon king, they brought with them an African giant,
called Colbrand, whom no ordinary man dare attack, until Guy, disguised as
an unknown Crusader, challenged and slew him.   After this feat he retired to
a cave near, still called Guy's Cliff, and lived and died a hermit, not even his
own wife knowing his real name and quality, but all this time awaiting his
return from the Holy Land.

Further down the Avon is Stratford, where is shown the old house where

Shakespeare, the greatest of all poets, was born ; and the clumsy oak school-desk where he sat learning to spell when a frolicsome school-boy. Here too is the church where he was buried, and there may still be seen the quaint lines which were written by his own desire over his humble grave.

By way of a contrast to the beauty and freshness of Warwickshire, let us step into the next county, Staffordshire, where all sorts of people are at work.

DUDLEY AT NIGHT, FROM THE OLD CASTLE WALLS.

Collieries and ironworks fill the air with smoke, while the busy potters have a district to themselves. Stoke-upon-Trent is called the mother of the potteries, though I think Burslem is the most central of the towns and villages which send cups, and pots, and pans all over the world.

The south part of this district is called the Black Country, for it is still more full of smoke ; even the very water is black with smoke and iron.

You must come with me to the top of this old castle of Dudley, first built among green woods and pleasant plains by Dodo the Saxon. See, from its grey walls we can get a view of the red chimneys of the busy town.

BATTLE-FIELD, SHREWSBURY.

"THE HOUSE IN THE FAIR WOOD."

Now, if you will like to hear of something else than smoke, come to Shropshire, through which flows the Severn, the largest river in England, and across
which, near Coalbrook Dale, is the first iron bridge ever made in England;
while in its neighbourhood is the first wooden railway. So you see it is worth
while to linger and look about us. Traces of some very old Roman roads
are visible in Shropshire; and at Wroxeter, near Shrewsbury, are the remains
of an ancient Roman city called Uriconium. The houses, the bath-rooms,
the roads, the market-place, have all been traced. Buried among the flues,

under a bath-room, was found the skeleton of an old man, who must have hidden there when the city was destroyed, and beside him lay a quantity of Roman coins; while on the dustheaps of the houses—the

REMAINS OF URICONIUM.

sweepings of some ancient drawing-rooms, where people sat and laughed and talked ever so many hundred years gone by—were found Roman buckles, hair-pins, needles, and coins, the whole telling the story of long-ago needs and fashions. Beyond Shrewsbury is Battle-field, near which is an old oak, nearly fifteen yards round, in which it is said the celebrated Glendower climbed to see the battle of Shrewsbury. It is quite hollow now; six people can stand inside it.

Of all stories connected with our quaint old English houses, there is not one more touching and romantic than that of Boscobel, "The house in the fair wood," a gaunt old two-storey mansion, built in the wilds of the neigh-bourhood, by John Giffard, a Roman Catholic gentleman, who had planned many an out-of-the-way hiding-place in his new mansion, where he might safely shelter persons of his own religion, who, in the troublous times of James I., had often been obliged to play hide and seek with justice and the ruling powers.

GLENDOWER'S OAK.

About the time I am speaking of, all England was aflame with the fierce struggle between king and people—"Cavaliers" and "Round-heads," as they were styled. There had been many battles, fought with varying success, and at last the "Roundheads" were triumphant. King Charles I. laid his head on the block at Whitehall, his wife and children were exiles, or prisoners in the land where they once were princes, and England was governed by Cromwell, the Protector.

Now a second Charles claimed the throne so rudely torn from his father; and history tells of the many fierce battles that took place—about these you can read in your school-books; the only one I want to interest you in is that of Worcester, fought on the 3rd of September, 1665. The young monarch, crowned King of Scotland, England, France, and Ireland, was but twenty-one years old when, entering the loyal city of Worcester with a small force, he prepared to encounter Cromwell's powerful host. It was a desperate chance. Some 2,000 English and 10,000 Scots, weary, harassed, and dispirited, against, perhaps, 30,000 picked troops, well provided with arms and ammunition—there seemed small possibility of success for the royal banner in fair open fight. So the young king determined to surprise the Parliamentary forces by attacking them unexpectedly at night, and 1,600 of his best men ventured forth on this forlorn hope; but they were betrayed by a tailor in the town, and the young king had to mourn the loss of many a brave follower ere the morning light dawned on the fatal anniversary of the Battle of Dunbar, where his father had been terribly defeated by Cromwell, who was wont to call this his "lucky day."

I am not going to describe the warlike deeds done by either side on that day—as I said, you will find all about it in your English History book. But I must tell you how the king and his most valued councillors met together on one of the towers of the cathedral, from whence they saw the Scotch troops below furiously attacked by General Lambert's army, while beyond was the invincible Cromwell himself, superintending the making of pontoon bridges, by which he could cross the Severn and attack the outposts of the town, which he presently did, with great masses of soldiers at his heels. On they came, slowly and steadily, at "push of pike," and the defenders of the town had to retreat in disorder, leaving only a long line of dead or wounded to hold good the outposts, while up there from the stone parapets of the old cathedral, the king and his council watched, with beating heart, the destruction of their troops. They saw through the thick smoke the wild struggle, the extreme peril of their friends below, and then they determined to sally forth themselves, sword in hand, and attack the enemy.

But it was all in vain, though Charles, dressed in armour himself, fought with most desperate valour. His Scotch troops gradually retreated, and were wedged in the streets of Worcester, with the enemy in hot pursuit. Soon they captured the cannon and turned them on the Royalists, who, at last, faint, and sorely discouraged and dismayed, strewing the streets with dead, turned to fly from the fatal city, in spite of the officers, who still tried to rally them, and the young king, who flung himself before them,

VIEW OF WORCESTER.

and cried aloud in his despair, "Shoot me through the head, and let me not see the consequences of this day!"

Yet even he had to confess further resistance would be useless. His best leaders were slain, his soldiers dead, dying, or flying before the fresh bands of merciless enemies pouring into the town. Those brave men who loved and honoured their prince most could but try to save him from fall ing into the hands of his furious enemies ; who, though elated with success, would have had little mercy on the Stuart. So a desperate rally was made by a faithful few, who fought round an overturned waggon at one end of the town, while the rest of the shattered host, flying for their lives, escaped through St. Martin's Gate, hurrying their bewildered prince away with them.

But as it is the fortunes of the distressed Charles Stuart we want to follow, we must leave the rest of our disheartened fugitives to their fate—only some 3,000 of all ranks escaped from Worcester—and tell what became of the forlorn young monarch himself.

Now there are two accounts as to the manner of his immediate escape, and as I cannot be quite sure which is the right one, I will give you both.

If we go to Worcester itself, we shall be told that Charles did not get away from it at once, in proof of which we shall be shown an old house in Friar Street, where it is said he was concealed. It is a kind of ware-house now, though over the entrance can still be seen, in quaint old letters, the motto, " Fear God, and honour the King, 1665." Moreover, we may have pointed out to us a huge old stone chimney, something like a staircase, up which we are told he scrambled, while the victorious Parliamentary troops were seeking him high and low, but he, with one guide, went safely over roof and parapet, until he was able to descend into a loyal citizen's house, and hence to another man's, who hid him in a kind of crypt, used by the then persecuted Roman Catholics as a chapel. From this extended passages, leading many ways, even to the vaults of the cathedral, and also to a house outside the town, which had once been a "white" nun's convent, and was, in consequence, still known as " White Ladies."

If you go to Worcester at any time, you ought certainly to visit this old mansion, where you will see the room in which it is said that the weary young fugitive rested for a time, until there was an alarm given that Parliamentary troopers were below in search of the king, whose track they had discovered. Then, in hot haste, he was roused from his slumbers, and having changed garments with his host and devoted adherent, Sir William Summers, he was lowered from the window in a blanket, and so in the end escaped from the clutches of his pursuers.

But now that I have told you what may be called " The Romance of

Worcester," let me give you the other, and, I believe, truer version of this most interesting story.

Charles, with the Earl of Derby, Colonel Roscarron, and sixty other gentlemen, escaped together in that dreadful rout, which seemed indeed, as the Puritans called it, "a setting of the king's glory." For many a weary mile they galloped gloomily and silently along, until in the dark stormy night they found themselves on a wild, deserted heath, near Kidderminster. Then the weary fugitives drew rein, and held a consultation as to what had better be done next.

The poor young king was very miserable and forlorn, cold, exhausted, and ready to drop with fatigue. Whatever else was decided on, it was evident that he must rest for a time. Rest, yes; but where? how? with Cromwell's fierce and victorious troops in hot pursuit behind them, and, may be, traitors before. In any case, it was a desperate venture. Then the Earl of Derby told how he had lately, after his defeat at Bolton-le-Moors, been hidden by some faithful, honest people in a strong house in Shropshire, full of hiding-places, called Boscobel, and that might still be a refuge for their fainting king.

It seemed a very dangerous refuge for the hunted prince to fly to, for its owner was, unluckily, no Royalist; but there was no time to hesitate. Charles desperately declared at once he would go, happen what might; and, fortunately for him, there stood forth a young cavalier among his jaded followers, who was a kinsman to the Puritan master of Boscobel, and who cheerfully offered to conduct him to this dangerous hiding-place, at whatever risk to himself. So they rode on, discoursing and holding counsel, until near Stourbridge they got a little bread and water for the hungry prince; and it was then arranged that it would be better for them all to stop together at some other place, the better to hide the fact of the young king's retreat to Boscobel. Then the same cavalier, young Giffard, told them of an old house, once a convent, called "White Ladies," which he thought would be safe for the present; and about forty of the party rode thither with the young leader they were so anxious to protect.

Giffard was well known at "White Ladies," and when they arrived at early dawn, he cheered the weary king by assuring him that he was safe for the present, and knocked at the door, which was opened by young George Penderel, son of William Penderel, the housekeeper, who must have started with surprise at the sight of the pale, worn faces and blood-stained garments of these early morning visitors. Then they hastily entered the inner parlour, and closing the doors, held anxious debate; all were weary, desperate, ruined men, in danger even of their very lives; but their principal anxiety was how to save their young king, who just now stood in such evil plight among them. The first and best thing to do, was to send for and confide in the Penderels—those honest brothers, who had so lately befriended the Earl of Derby. They soon came in, wondering, and the earl, taking the young king's hand, said solemnly to one of them, who stood looking on in amazement, " See, honest William Penderel, this is thy king and mine! thou must have a care of him, and preserve him, as thou didst me." And William, looking up with his blue eyes—honest and true—simply answered, that he would do so, " God permitting." A strange scene followed, for the first thing to be done was to alter the appearance of the royal fugitive, and there were few means at hand, or scant time for ceremony. Richard Penderel having no scissors, cut, or rather hacked, off the king's flowing black ringlets with a woodman's bill which he happened to have in his belt; then he suggested that his majesty was dark-complexioned certainly, but not dark enough, so he rubbed his hands in the soot of the chimney, and smeared and blackened his skin as much as he could; then he took off his buff coat, and delicately-laced ruff, the broad blue ribbon from his breast, the badge of the garter, and all other things he had worn so long, and put on a coarse shirt belonging to a servant of the house, then Richard's own green suit and leather doublet. It was all done in hot haste, for it was said there was a troop of Parliamentary soldiers but three miles off, who might arrive and detect the party at any moment; as it was, they did arrive exactly half an hour after their bird had flown. And now came the sorrowful time of parting; would they ever meet again—the old and tried lords and the disguised boy prince they had staked and lost their all for? Few and sorrowful were the words exchanged as Richard let him out of a back door, and only very few went with him as far as Spring Coppice, and there bade him a sad farewell; leaving him in the care of these trusty but humble brothers, who, fortunately, had no thought to betray their master.

Then the Earl of Derby and the rest of the party, led by Charles Giffard, mounted in haste, and trotted towards the town of Newport, but there they were followed and stopped by the enemy's forces. The loyal earl who surrendered on promise of quarter, and had thought more of saving his king than of hiding himself at Boscobel, as he might have so easily done, was tried at once by his captors, and beheaded. Fortunately, young Giffard escaped, with many others, from the inn where he was imprisoned.

But let us leave the scene of blood and vengeance, and return to the

BOSCOBEL HOUSE.

flowery glades of Spring Coppice, where the sun was slowly rising, while the heavy rain came pouring down in torrents, so that even the thick foliage could not shelter the poor young king and his new protectors. By this time Charles was too weary to stand; but there was no place here to rest on, so Richard ran to a neighbour's house and borrowed an old blanket, which he folded, and made in that damp place into a sorry seat—a poor throne for the throneless, homeless heir of three realms. The young Puritan woman of whom Richard had borrowed the blanket was his sister-in-law. He felt she might and must be trusted, so he asked her to make him some breakfast, and bring it to him at such a place in the wood—a strange request on a pouring wet morning, but these were strange times—and the housewife asked no questions, but presently came through the glade well laden with hot milk, bread and butter, and eggs. The king was sitting half starved with cold and hunger, yet when he heard her he started up, with the terror of being discovered and betrayed. He looked in the kind, compassionate, womanly face before him, and cried, forgetting that, to all appearance, he was only a swarthy woodman, "Good woman, can you be faithful to a distressed cavalier in danger of his life?" and she answered simply, as the Penderels had done, "Yes, sir; I would die rather than discover you." Then the young man sat down with a lightened heart, and enjoyed the welcome meal, simple as it was. I dare say, never in his days of greatest splendour did anything taste as good as that plain food, eaten under the dripping shades of Spring Coppice, with those poor, true subjects looking pityingly on. Refreshed and strengthened, he next planned to leave this retreat and get away to Wales, if possible. Richard promised to guide him, but first took him to his own humble home, Habbal Grange, where he introduced him to his old mother, Dame Penderel, whose eldest son had died fighting in the service of King Charles I., and whose remaining five would have risked life and limb in the Stuarts' service. Here the young king's disguise was made as complete as possible. Richard was a plain woodman, and Charles was to pretend to be his servant; he was furnished with big clouted shoes and a woodman's bill; then they waited for the night to set in, and started for Madeley, about five miles off, near the river Severn, which the party would have to cross to get into Wales.

Often in that weary walk did the prince (who, by-the-by, was to be called Will Jones) have to stop and take off those heavy clouted shoes, which made his blistered feet ache at every step, and walk barefoot. Once, in passing Evelin Mill, Richard let a gate clap too behind them, and the gruff miller came staring about, and asking crossly, "Who's there?" Richard, who did not care to answer the question, dragged the king through a brook, which filled the unlucky shoes full of water, and made them ten times more unbearable than before; added to which, it was so dark that, to use Charles' own words, "the rustling of Richard's calf-skin breeches was the best direction he had to follow him in that dark night, when one could not see a hand before one." Little did the anxious pair think that within that very mill

I. THE PROSCRIBED ROYALIST.

which they passed in the silence and darkness of night were assembled a party of Royalists, and that the dreaded miller was only keeping guard, that they might not be surprised by any lurking foe.

At length, about midnight, they arrived at Madeley, where dwelt a right loyal gentleman, named Woolf. Of course they decided to go at once to his place; but all the household had retired to rest. What was to be done? They dared not linger about, so Richard knocked long and steadily at the door, until the voice of Miss Woolf wonderingly asked who was without, seeking admittance at so late an hour; and Richard Penderel's voice, which she well knew, whispered back, "Hush! 'tis the king!"

A strange, startling announcement to be heard at one's own door at a time when to be known as a Royalist brought death and disgrace to all—when military executions were common in the neighbourhood. Yet Richard had judged the family aright; they never shrunk from the danger and risk, but received their dangerous visitor as an honoured and welcome guest.

Yet but a short time was there for the fugitive to rest and refresh in this hospitable mansion; the wary enemy kept strict charge of the passage of the Severn; and as a party of Cromwell's people were expected to pass through the town, it was possible and likely that they would quarter themselves in this very house; so "Will Jones" and his master retreated to the big barn, where they stayed, quietly concealed, all next day.

After all the venture and risk of the journey, it was judged too great a risk to attempt to cross into Wales, and Mr. Woolf persuaded them to return for a time to the safer depths of Boscobel. He hurried them away from their present dangerous hiding-place, his wife having first stained the king's still delicate hands with walnut-juice. And so at midnight the weary march back was resumed. The poor young prince was so overcome with disappointment and pain, for his swollen and blistered feet would scarcely carry him, that when about half-way he flung himself on the cold, damp ground, declaring life was not worth the trouble of preserving, and that he would rather die than suffer thus. Perhaps he would have died had not the good and faithful Richard comforted him with words of patience, hope, and future fortune; and so, partly by coaxing, partly by dragging, got him on to his feet, and once more on their way to Boscobel, where at last they arrived at about three o'clock in the morning. Even then they could not go at once into the house, for fear of Cromwell's soldiers, so Charles hid in the wood, while Richard went first to see if all were safe. How thankful they were to find only William, his wife, and a loyal Colonel Carliss, who was also hiding in the friendly shades of "The house in the fair wood."

So the three went out in the dark night to meet the king, who was sitting, in a melancholy mood, on the trunk of a tree; there was a greeting, and then they all returned within doors to a famous feast of bread and cheese. "My Dame Joan," as the king called her, made him a posset of new milk and small beer, which warmed the poor chilled body of the luckless wanderer, while Colonel Carliss took off the clouted shoes and torn, wet stockings, and gently bathed his royal master's feet, until he felt quite comforted.

But all this time the talk was about hiding him again, for the Round-head troopers were round and about everywhere in search of Charles. Humphrey Penderel had yesterday encountered an officer, who had some suspicion that the king was in hiding near. He had examined Penderel, and told him that whoever concealed him would be shot without mercy. The reward for giving him up was pardon for all else, and a thousand pounds down.

A thousand golden guineas—a great sum to tempt a poor miller! a word or hint would have gained them, but Humphrey only shook his head and looked so vacant, that he was let go on his way unsuspected, while he hurried back to tell the news of the soldier's suspicions, and the value set on the life of the king, who sat among them with a pale face and weak heart, wondering what was to follow.

He could not stay in Boscobel House, suspected as it was; he could not hide or escape in time; what then was to be done?

All round about flourished grand old trees; and some one thought of hiding the king in one of them, a huge foliage-covered oak, that stood in great state near the house. A cushion was laid across some branches, and here the king and colonel passed the hours, shaded by the green leaves; it was no bad resting-place—the first quiet one he had been in for days. So the young fugitive stretched himself as well as he could, and laying his head—worth a thousand pounds to any one who could point it out, for all it looked so ragged and unkempt—on Colonel Carliss's friendly knee, the homeless, crownless king slept peacefully for hours, forgetting all his troubles, perils, and dangerous position.

Slowly the day wore away, and the soft twilight came on; the little birds singing their evening carol must have wondered what strange creatures were these in the branches, hiding in their domains. The king still slept, while his guardian sat stiff and still for fear of arousing him. Suddenly the silence was broken, for there came a great band of troopers, followed by a crowd of dogs, all barking and baying; the men had tracked the king, first to "White Ladies," then to Boscobel. But their search was in vain. They looked in every nook and corner—everywhere except above their heads in the thick green branches, where their prey was hid—then they rode off at last; and present safety being restored, it was decided to hide Charles in a secret recess—the very same where the Earl of Derby had once been concealed. So Dame Joan put a bed in it, and William cut his tangled hair properly with a pair of scissors, though, as Colonel Carliss said, "he made but a mean barber;" and then they had supper of chickens. So dainty a dish the king and the colonel had not tasted for a long time; you may think how they enjoyed it!

"Now, your majesty," asked the colonel, laughingly, after supper, "mention what you would like for your Sunday dinner."

"Mutton, if I could get it," answered the king.

So they determined that mutton he should have; but how? There was none to be had about there; so the colonel went to a fold near by, and killed a sheep, which Will Penderel carried home on his back; so the king had his mutton after all.

I must not forget to tell you that honest William was not long before he went to the owner of it, and telling under what necessity he had helped himself to the sheep, offered to pay for it; but the kindly Mr. Stanton only laughed, and said he was glad that the king had tasted his mutton—he was only too welcome to it.

Next day, which was Sunday, Charles, who could not get rest very well in his hiding-place, was seen praying very fervently in the little gallery near it; by-and-by he merrily assisted the colonel to cook some mutton chops for their dinner. How often, in after life, when he sat at the grand feasts he was fond of indulging in, he must have remembered how great a luxury such a dinner as this had seemed! There he sat quietly on this sober Sunday evening reading, or listening to the songs of the birds, and smelling the sweet scent of the flowers that clustered round a pretty arbour in the gardens. He seemed almost happy that day; yet all this time the three Penderel

THE STORY OF THE OLD OAK.

brothers kept strict watch, lest any troopers should approach the place unawares.

And now he must leave this shelter for another, as news was brought by John Penderel, that Lord Wilmot was safe at the house of Mr. Whitgreave of Mosely, and trusted the king would come to them at once.

As he could not attempt another long walk, it was arranged that he should mount the mill horse; so he bade adieu to Colonel Carliss, who dare not show himself at Mosely; and at twelve o'clock rode through a drenching thunder-storm, followed by the good brothers Penderel and their brother

A CAVALIER FAMILY.

in-law, all well armed and resolute men, determined to protect their master to the death.

It was not by any means easy work riding on this old mill horse. "Truly," exclaimed the king, who was almost jogged to pieces, "this is the heaviest, dullest jade that I ever bestrode!" And Humphrey, the miller, laughed as he answered, jokingly, "My liege, you cannot blame the mare for going slowly, when she carries the weight of three kingdoms on her back!"

At last they reached Mr. Whitgreave's house; Richard and John were to stay with the king, the other brothers were to return to Boscobel. The king, not knowing this, was entering the house hurriedly, when he saw his true men departing silently one by one; then he turned back in haste, and, holding out his darkened hand to them, exclaimed, " My troubles make me forget myself. I thank you all from my heart!"

Then he entered the room where Lord Wilmot had been waiting in fear and trembling, lest the king might be captured on his way. When he saw his prince in safety, he flung himself on his knees in an agony of thankfulness, and caught him in his arms, weeping like a child; the young king put his arms around his friend and kissed his cheek, and asked, hurriedly, " Wilmot, where are the others—Buckingham, Cleveland ?"

But Wilmot could not answer; where, indeed? he could only turn to Mr. Whitgreave, and say to him, " This is my master, the master of us all."

This the master of them all! What a strange figure he looked—in old leathern doublet, muddy green breeches, and a short " jump coat," a pair of stockings with the embroidered tops cut off, the old clouted shoes all cut and slashed to make them endurable, a greasy old grey hat, and common coarse shirt. Once his nose began to bleed, and he pulled out such a rag of a handkerchief, that those present looked at each other in horror and dismay; but it did not seem to trouble " the master" much. So they brought him a clean linen shirt, and dried his poor wet feet; and soon he rested in a narrow hole of a hiding-place, where he slept, and forgot all his troubles for the time.

Next day, as he sat in a kind of cupboard over the porch, where he could see all those who approached the house, he was horrified to observe a party of Roundhead soldiers—but, luckily, they had not come in search of him, but to arrest Mr. Whitgreave, charging him with having fought in the Royalist army at Worcester.

Fortunately, this was really not true; and the generous host, having first securely hid his guest, went to the soldiers, and proved to them that he had not been out of the house for a fortnight, and at last they went away, little dreaming how near they were to earning a thousand pounds.

Later on in the day came two other alarms, in the shape of two bands of soldiers, who searched the house, devoured all they could find, offered to shoot William Penderel, and frightened " my Dame Joan" almost out of her wits. Then they took themselves off to "White Ladies," and searched and smashed all before them, but, of course, with no success.

Now there was a Mrs. Jane Lane, a sister of a friend of Lord Wilmot's, who had a pass from the Commander for herself and groom to go to Bristol, where her sister was lying ill. Here was a famous chance for Lord Wilmot to escape as her groom, but he gave it up, without a sigh, in favour of his royal friend and master.

KITCHEN OF THE 17TH CENTURY.

And so in the cold night Colonel Lane came to the orchard corner, and carried away the king, that he might join his wife. "Farewell!" said the grateful prince, as his preservers pressed round him with tears and good wishes, "if ever God restores me to my dominions, I will not be unmindful of your services." And he well remembered that promise in the days of his restoration.

When Charles arrived at Bentley with Colonel Lane, of course he had to behave as a rough groom, and sat down by the kitchen fire in as sulky and clownish a fashion as he could assume.

"Here, you idle fellow!" cried the cook, "just watch that this roast meat does not burn ; make yourself useful, will you ? and attend to that joint, and turn the spit." This picture will show you how meat was roasted then.

Presently a sneaking sort of fellow, a spy in reality, came poking about the large kitchen, to see and hear all he could. Seeing a strange face at the fireside, he sidled up to the new groom, and began asking all sorts of questions, while staring hard at him. Luckily, one of the servants, who was in the secret, and on the watch, came forward, and before the disguised king had time to answer, gave him two or three sounding blows on the head with the basting-ladle, and calling him all the bad names he could think of, ordered him to mind his business, which was to keep the

MRS. LANE AND HER NEW SERVING-MAN.

spit going, and not to prate to every passer-by. So seeing the storm he had raised, and afraid of the hot ladle, the other fellow took himself off, and Charles was once more safe for the time being.

Thus well disguised as a humble serving-man, Charles escorted Mrs. Lane on her journey, she riding on a pillion behind him, as was the custom of the time, while Lord Wilmot followed slowly at a distance, ready to give the alarm. Fortunately no alarm was needed.

When they arrived at the lady's house at Bristol, "the man" led the horse to the stable, and having attended to it, loudly declared that he felt so agueish, that he would go to bed at once. This he did to avoid dangerous company; but, as ill-luck would have it, the butler, who had been a soldier in the service of Charles I., thinking the strange servant was ill, kindly brought him up some refreshment, and looking in the white, worn, young face, he recognised it instantly, and, with tearful eyes, fell on his knees, exclaiming in right eager fashion, " I am rejoiced to see your majesty safe!" Here was an unforeseen danger; but his first excitement over, the good old servant kept the secret bravely, and with his help, and that of brave Mrs. Lane and others, the royal fugitive was hidden until the end of October, when he managed to escape from Shoreham, in Sussex, to the safer coast of Dieppe, where he was landed in safety at last. The thousand pounds offered by Parliament, a goodly sum in those days, did not induce one of the many—some very poor and humble folks—who knew of his whereabouts, to betray the fugitive prince.

But now for a brighter scene, where we shall see—

> " The man of Boscobel
> In different guise, I ween, from what he was
> When blood-hounds bayed around the royal oak,
> And the white owl flew forth and shrieked aloud
> Her angry malison on those who scanned
> The guardian tree, thirsting for royal blood,
> And marked the umbrageous leaves and branches shake;
> Then cried—
>   ' Away, 'twas but yon sullen bird
>   Our dogs have startled from its secret haunt,
>   And not the man we seek, whose outlawed head
>   Were worth its weight in gold.'
>   And so passed on.
> Unconscious of the quarry lodged so near."

WHITEHALL PALACE IN THE DAYS OF THE STUARTS.

Long years afterwards, when King Charles, surrounded by courtiers and splendour of every kind, stood once more in Whitehall Palace, he sent for all those faithful brothers, still living in their quiet home in Shropshire, and having thanked them publicly and most gratefully for their services, offered them any favour in his power to grant. But they only asked that they and theirs, being Roman Catholics, might be left in peace. With the promise of this, and a moderate pension, which the king determined they should have, they returned quite content and happy.

When, long afterwards, Charles II. visited "The house in the fair woods" of Shropshire, I think he must have thanked God, who had saved him from past perils, and given him such a loyal people. It is said that he looked very serious as he stood under the "Royal Oak," thinking, most likely, of the days

> "When Penderel, the miller, at risk of his blood,
> Hid the king of the isle in the king of the wood."

His majesty carried away with him a few acorns, which he himself carefully planted in St. James's Park. In time a tree sprang from one of them, which he often tended and watered with his own hands; it flourished in sight of his chamber window, on the site of Marlborough House, where our Prince of Wales lives. It was called the "King's Royal Oak," and long reminded passers-by of

> "The 29th of May,
> The Royal Oak day,

VIEW OF NOTTINGHAM.

NOTTINGHAM.

LET us not miss taking a peep at this old town, and its close and noisy bustling neighbourhood, where so many people are busy in their small cottages, weaving cotton stockings or making bobbin net, two things for which Nottingham is famous. On an almost perpendicular rock, 133 feet high, stands the ruin of a comparatively modern building. Once on the same spot stood the strongest castle in the Midland counties—the bulwark of the Crown in all cases of emergency. There are secret passages in that tall, dark, sandstone rock, and one, which visitors can visit, is called "Mortimer's Hole." We find its story in our "History of England;" if we open it at the beginning of

NOTTINGHAM CASTLE.

the reign of King Edward III., we may read all about it. Mortimer, the
ambitious, wicked favourite of Isabella, the self-made widow of Edward II.,
was by her means made Earl of March and Regent of England. He so
angered the nobles, and even the young king—whom he treated as a baby,
although now eighteen years of age—by his insolent and cruel conduct, that
they tried in every way to bring him to justice, knowing that he had accom-
plished the late king's death.

But the bad queen retired with him into the strong castle of Nottingham.
She every night had the keys of the fortress put under her pillow, and as

IN THE SECRET PASSAGE.

gunpowder was not used, and the rock was well guarded and inaccessible, it seemed likely enough that the young king might wait outside long enough before this bad man, protected by a foolish queen, would surrender.

However, the governor of the castle was won over, and young Edward's soldiers, under Lord Montacute, were led through a secret subterranean passage to a room where the wicked Earl of March was quietly conversing with some friends, quite unprepared for the peril awaiting him.

MORTIMER'S HOLE.

He was at once seized, two of his guards were slain, and the queen rushing in, flung herself at the king's feet, crying, "Fair son, have pity on my gentle Mortimer!" But the young king knew too well the worth of the Earl of March, and would not listen to her entreaties on his behalf. He was hurried away down this "Mortimer's Hole" so quietly and secretly, that the very guards on the ramparts knew nothing of his arrest, and the next day found himself in the Tower of London, and soon afterwards at Smithfield, where he was executed, A.D. 1330.

"IN THE MERRY GREEN WOOD."

SHERWOOD FOREST AND ROBIN HOOD.

HONOUR to the old bow string;
Honour to the bugle horn ;
Honour to the woods unshorn;
Honour to the Lincoln green ;
Honour to the archer keen ;
Honour to light " Little John,"

And the horse he rode upon ;
Honour to bold Robin Hood,
Sleeping in the underwood ;
Honour to Maid Marian,
And to all the Sherwood clan.

Keats.

" Bold Robin Hood was a forester good
As ever drew bow in the merry green wood."

WE cannot pass by where once was Sherwood Green without being
reminded of that famous outlaw, Robin Hood, or Robin o' th' Wood, and
although we have all heard something of him, I think we may linger a few
moments to recall his story, so often said and sung, but always interesting, for
the merry pranks he played would take an age to tell. Some say that Robin

M

never existed, except in poet's fancy. I don't want to believe them, do you? He was born at Locksley, when King Henry II. ruled the land. His real name was Robert or Robin Fitzooth. Some add that he was really Earl of Huntingdon, but of that I cannot be quite sure. All I am sure of is, that he was a wild and extravagant youth, though active, honourable, and brave, who ate and drank away all his inheritance, and then was outlawed for debt. Such things happen even in these matter-of-fact days, only now people cannot very well do as Robin did—seek an asylum in green woods and dense forests of oaks and elms, such as in those times covered the northern parts of England, and where he seems to have led a happy, joyous, free life, in company with several other persons, who accepted him as their leader, being much in the same plight as his scapegrace self. How well we know the names of that joyous band in Lincoln green: there were " bold Will Scarlet," and " George a' Green," and " Friar Tuck," not forgetting " fair Maid Marian," and " Little John : "

> " Though he was called little, his limbs they were large,
> And his stature was seven feet high,
> Wheresoever he came they quaked at his name,
> For soon he would make them to fly."

Altogether this free company of the woods at last amounted to more than a hundred archers, well practised with the long bow and other weapons of the time, so bold and skilful, that four times the number of ordinary men dared not attack them. They feasted right royally on the forest deer, which then abounded, and they took what else they required from the wealthy travellers whom they waylaid, or by fair commerce. When they were too much opposed or molested in one place, they retreated to another ; and as they were ever kindly disposed and good to the poor and needy, sharing with rather than taking from them, no wonder that the forces that were every now and then sent out against them always returned home empty-handed and discomfited.

Even those who have styled Robin Hood a robber, add that he was the Prince of Robbers, for he and his fellows never killed or hurt any one, or ill-treated women or poor people. The rich clergy of the times they held in great abhorrence, and played them many a trick, as we may read in the old ballads.

And thus for many years he kept up a sort of independent sovereignty in the green glades about Nottinghamshire, setting magistrates, soldiers, and all others at defiance. So that at last a royal proclamation was published, and a great reward offered to any one who would bring him a prisoner to Henry III., for he was reigning then; but no one claimed the bribe, no one would betray brave bold Robin Hood.

But at length the woodland king grew very sick, and he went for aid and advice to his own kinswoman, the prioress of Kirklees Nunnery, in Yorkshire; for in those days, when nuns and monks led a much quieter life than any one else, they studied medicine, understood herbs and surgery, and gave help to those requiring it; so no wonder that when this lady told him very gravely that he required bleeding, true-hearted Robin believed her, and submitted his arm to her lancet, little dreaming that she would be treacherous enough to let him bleed to death before her eyes.

Some traditions say that, as he felt himself dying, he called for his bow, and letting fly an arrow, chose the place where he desired to be buried.

> " Give me my bent bow in my hand,
> And a broad arrow I'll let flee ;
> And where the arrow is taken up,
> There shall my grave digged be.
>
> " Lay me a green sod under my head,
> And another under my feet ;
> And lay my bent bow by my side,
> Which was my music sweet ;
> And make my grave of gravel and green,
> Which is most right and meet.
>
> " Let me have length and breadth enough,
> With a green sod under my head,
> That they may say when I am dead—
> ' Here lies bold Robin Hood.'
>
> " These words they readily promised him,
> Which did bold Robin please ;
> And there they buried bold Robin Hood,
> Near to the fair Kirklees."

Near Sherwood is Mansfield, about which we are told that when King Henry II. had been hunting in the forest, he wandered away to this place, and meeting a miller, begged a meal of him. The good man, little knowing with whom he was dealing, not only gave Henry supper, but a bed also, and treated him very kindly. Next morning, before the guest rose, there came a great crowd inquiring anxiously for the king. The miller took no notice, and was as much surprised as any one when he heard a voice calling from his window, "I am here!"

THE BREAD STONE, EAST RETFORD.

We have all read of the great plagues that in old times ravaged England, more particularly London, especially that of 1665. We know how soon houses began to empty and graves began to fill; how the pious words, "Lord, have mercy upon us!" scrawled in a great crimson cross, too often appeared on doors, to warn passers-by that the pestilence was doing or

THE FIRST HOUSE SMITTEN BY THE PLAGUE
ASHLIN'S PLACE, DRURY LANE.

had done its work within; while the deserted streets echoed with the solemn cry, "Bring out your dead! bring out your dead!" No longer were the open shops filled with finery; and no more did the bustling, busy dealer walk up and down showing his wares, and crying, "What d'ye lack?" All those who could, fled the stricken city. They fled in crowds into the country places, until the neighbouring towns and villages refused to receive them for fear of contagion. Poor things! money availed them little; men, women, and children had to encamp in the open fields—a Londoner was more dreaded than a wild beast. The country folk would have no dealings with them, for they dared not take their money, for fear it might carry infection with it. So the poor fugitives were sorely troubled, and seemed to have fled from pestilence to starvation. At last resort was had to a mode of barter, a monument of which remains in the Bread Stone, near the pretty town of East Retford, Nottinghamshire. It was arranged that the dreaded wanderer should place the price of what food he might require on a huge stone that stood at a safe distance from the town; that he should then retire; and after the coins had lain there some hours to purify, the trader should replace them with the much-needed provisions.

VORK.

YORKSHIRE.

YORK, York, for my money,
Of all the cities that ever I see,
For merry pastime and company,
    Except the city of London.

God save the Queen and keep the peace.
That our good shooting may increase ;

And praying to God, let us not cease,
    As well at York as at London,

That all our country round about,
May have archers good to hit the clout,
Which England cannot be without,
    No more than York or London.
                        Old Ballad

As we approach the fine county town of York—near which, by-the-by, I am told, the famous Guy Fawkes, "please to remember the fifth of November, gunpowder treason and plot" man was born—we pass through great fields of golden-coloured mustard plants, or of stiff prickly-looking teazle—a kind of thistle, used to prepare the surface of cloth: oddly enough, it does this far better than any machinery could—and at last we come to a fine wall that has four gates. This wall can tell how old and famous the place is, for it was built by the Romans, who, in the "once upon a time," made York their capital, and called it Eboracum. Here two of their emperors died, and it is said to have been the birth-place of the famous Constantine the Great, the first Christian emperor.

But I wanted to tell you about the old Emperor Severus. He it was who, while living at York, employed his army to build a great stone wall, stretching across the island from the Solway to the mouth of the Tyne, and which was not finished until A. D. 210, and is still called by his name. It was seventy-eight miles long, twelve feet high, and eight feet wide, with towers and fortresses to strengthen it in case of assault. At one time, when this emperor was very ill, his wicked son, Caracalla—who had already tried to poison him, failed, and been forgiven—prevailed on his father's soldiers to desert the poor old emperor, saying "that as he had something the matter with his feet, he was unfit to govern!" So, by means of fine promises and gifts, he persuaded many to proclaim him in his father's stead. His baseness met with its due reward, for his forces were defeated, and himself taken prisoner, and brought before his justly-offended father, before whose throne he threw himself, begging for forgiveness—not that he was sorry or ashamed, only afraid of being punished.

"What!" exclaimed the unhappy father, bitterly; "have you yet to learn that it is the head, and not the feet, that govern men?" Severus died at York, which the Romans had made so flourishing, for, as you may have read, the towns of the ancient Britons were only clusters of huts, fortified by a row of felled trees and a deep ditch ; but under the Romans the country prospered, and when they left it, it possessed more than fifty walled towns; and besides, there were many military stations, baths, temples, public buildings, and even a theatre large enough to hold two or three thousand persons.

In York there is a fine old castle, now used as a gaol ; and one of the finest

YORK MINSTER.

cathedrals in England, in which are some very interesting monuments of our early kings.

We cannot wander round the coast of Yorkshire without noticing two important capes—one called Flamborough Head, or rather "the head with a flame," so called on account of the beacon fire that used to burn there in old times; and the other called Sperm Head. The former is very high, and formed of brilliant white chalk; whilst the latter is a long, low ridge tapering to a point, and formed of sand and shingle.

The sea washes away every year about two yards of this shore, all the way between Bridlington Bay and this Sperm Head, and then it washes back all this mass of soil into the Humber, so that some land called Sunk Island, which, in the reign of Charles I., was only a mud bank in the middle of the river, now forms a part of the main land, and is covered with corn-fields, meadows, cottages, and farm buildings, pleasant to look upon.

Strolling along about Flamborough Head, we see great wave-dashed rocks, where many thousands

GATHERING SEA-BIRDS' EGGS.

of sea-birds swarm, laying countless numbers of eggs, which are eagerly sought for by men and boys, who risk their lives in the search. Let us watch these two men who, standing out on the great cliffs, are preparing to descend its steep side in search of the greenish-blue eggs of the Guil lemot, lying on the bare hard rocks, or the spotted ones of the Kittewake, lying in countless numbers of nests of dried grasses, far below any ridge where you would like to venture.

The men drive an iron bar deep into the ground, and to this bar they tie a thick rope, which is flung over the rocks; then one man slips into a pair of rope braces, which meet round him so as to form a kind of waistband, and through the end of this is passed a loop-hole, through which is drawn a smaller rope, which the other man holds firmly, while he gradually lowers his comrade over the steep and dangerous cliff; and so clinging on to the rope

GULLS.

fastened to the bar, he at last reaches the ledges where the nests are laid, and picks up the eggs as fast as he can.

In some parts of the coast, especially as we go on farther north, we see still greater numbers of these wild sea-birds darting by, some skimming low on the waters, seeking for food, others wheeling round in great clouds. What are they? Great white Gulls of many kinds, all fond of herrings, and following the shoals so diligently; Puffins and the Sea-Mews, which come sometimes inland in large flocks, looking almost like sea foam as they settle down on the newly-ploughed earth, seeking for worms; the Fulmar, which builds its nest on the face of the highest precipices, and which forms the only riches of the poor inhabitants of some of the islands round about St. Kilda, who daily risk their necks in pursuit of the one white egg which the bird lays in its nest; but then these nests lie close and thick on the rocks, and the bodies of the parent birds supply fat and oil   See, here are some Petrels, of different

WRECKED ON THE YORKSHIRE COAST.

kinds; when they are searching for food, they fly close to the surface of the waves, and pat the water just as though they were running on it. Some call them " Peters " because of this, in reference to the Apostle Peter walking on the waves.

Sailors detest the smaller kind, which is known as the Stormy Petrel; they call it "Mother Cary's Chicken." Who Mother Cary was I do not know, nor do I know why her chickens should have meant coming storm and tempest when they appeared in the wake of a ship; but it is most likely they come before a gale for shelter. At any rate, it is not strange they should be thought birds of evil omen, and dreaded as such.

A PEEP FROM THE SEA.

SCARBOROUGH.

A little to the north of Flamborough Head stands Scarborough, called the "queen of watering-places," and the first thing we must notice is the ruin of its once proud castle. This brave old fortress, built in the reign of King Stephen, stands on the summit of the bold cliff or "scar," from which it took its name; and see, the town, now so fashionable and busy, has little by little crept almost up to it, but at first it was content to cluster here and there a few houses down on the sands at its feet, and its inhabitants were mostly fishers.

> "Castle of ancient days! in times long gone,
> Thy lofty halls in royal splendour shone;
> Thou stood'st, a monument of strength, sublime—
> A giant, laughing at the threats of time.
> Strange scenes have passed within thy walls, and strange
> Has been thy fate through many a chance and change!
> Thy towers have heard the war-cry, and the shout
> Of friends within and answering foes without
> Have rung to sounds of revelry, while mirth
> Held her carousal."

It has been very famous in the old fighting times, when its story was one of resistance and warfare. Robert Bruce burnt the town, and later on, when a daring Scotch cattle freebooter was at last captured and sent to strong old Scarborough for safety, his son came with ships and determined men, and carried off many merchant-vessels from out of the harbour, so they soon had to give up their prisoner again. Richard "Crookback" visited the town, and, I suppose, liked it, for he made it into a county of itself, but it did not retain that dignity long.

Perhaps you have heard of "a Scarborough warning"—that is, a word and a blow, but the blow comes first. That saying took its rise from the time of Elizabeth, when a son of Lord Stafford surprised and took the castle, not by assault, but by introducing into it a number of armed men dressed like peasants. However, in three days the Earl of Westmorland retook it, and at once executed young Stafford and his followers, without listening to anything they had to urge. He had no time to waste, and said they must explain afterwards.

Much later on, when the place had been dismantled, but was still used as a prison, George Fox, the first of the Quakers, was imprisoned and very hardly used here; the officers of the place often threatened him with hanging, telling him the king had ordered him there on account of the great interest he had with the people, and that if any insurrection occurred he would be hung over the prison wall as a terror to others. But he only answered, that he was ready, fearing neither death nor suffering, in God's name. Truly—

> "Stone walls do not a prison make,
> Nor iron bars a cage."

Siege-pieces were a kind of token-money, used during the fighting times of the Commonwealth, when King Charles was driven from town to town, and from castle to castle. His treasures became exhausted, his royal purse empty, and even the household plate was sold or melted.

Then his loyal adherents gave their gold and silver plate to be cut up and stamped in some rude fashion, and so made into a kind of money. These new-fashioned coins, often showing the mouldings of the salvers of which they had formed part, were called siege-pieces, or money of necessity, and on some we can make out the rough effigy of the castle or town where they were issued.

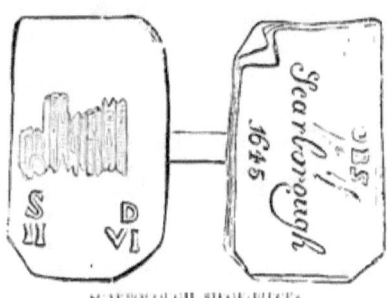

SCARBOROUGH SIEGE-PIECES.

About a mile from the sea, between two brooks, we can see the remains of the desolate old castle of Mulgrave, all covered with ivy. About this place, too, there are some quaint traditions told, such as these, for instance—I leave you to believe as much of them as you like :—

"In the building of Mulgrave and Pickering Castles, Duke Wada, or Wade, and his wife Bell, divided the work, a single one of these giants being strong enough to rear the building required ; but having, unfortunately, only one hammer between them, they were obliged to keep tossing it backwards and forwards, giving a loud shout every time, that when the one threw it to Mulgrave or to Pickering, the other might be ready to catch it. What is really a Roman road, but which is called 'Wade's Causey,' or 'Wade's Wife's Causey,' was formed by them in a very short time, Bell fetching the stones, and Wade laying them down. Now and then her apron-strings broke, and the large heap of stones here and there still show the places where the stones fell. Young Master Wade, even when a baby, could throw a rock weighing several tons to a vast distance ; and one day, when his mother was milking her cow some miles off, he threw a huge stone that grazed the good lady slightly, but made such an impression on the hard rock, that it could be seen marked and broken where it was struck, the stone itself being splintered in pieces, and its remains scattered far and near."

WHITBY.

This ancient town owes its origin to Oswy, King of Northumberland, who once made a vow that if God would grant him victory over the Pagan King

FOSSIL AMMONITE.

of Mercia, he would found a monastery here, and devote his baby-daughter to a life of retirement within its walls.

Lady Hilda, its first abbess, was renowned for her goodness and sanctity. Tradition tells of the wonders she did ; one marvel, especially, regarding the many curious fossil ammonites which abound in the neighbourhood—little curled-up stony things, such as many of you may have seen. These, folks say, were once living snakes, which infested Whitby, doing much harm, but which, by the prayers of this holy woman, were all driven over the steep cliff into the sea, each one having its neck broken in the fall.

Another tale is, that some sea-fowl, flying over the convent, were so attracted by its holy occupant, that they all sank to the ground, unable to proceed any further. Sir Walter Scott's two nuns tell how—

> " In their convent cell
> A Saxon princess once did dwell,
>   The lovely Edelfled ;
> And how of thousand snakes, each one
> Was changed into a coil of stone
>   When holy Hilda prayed.
> Themselves, within their holy bound,
> Their stony folds had often found ;
> They told how sea-fowls' pinions fail
> As over Whitby's towers they sail :
> And sinking down, with fluttering faint,
>   They do their homage to the saint."

The cliffs round about here are very steep, and in the neighbourhood a

WHITBY ABBEY.

great deal of alum is found. A quantity of jet is dug out of the rocks; it is found in thin masses, and manufactured into beads and brooches, to be sent all over the world; for Whitby jet is famous everywhere.

A curious service used to be performed by the owners of certain lands hereabouts on the morning of Ascension Day. They erected, in a particular part of the harbour, a small hedge or fence of slender posts driven into the ground, and secured by hazels twisted in and out, like wicker-work. While this was being done, the bailiff of the lord of the manor looked on, and a man, blowing a horn, called out every now and then, while the hedge was making, "Out on you; out on you!"—a curious old custom, that some say arose from the custom of the tenants of the abbey lands belonging to the convent, though others believe it to have been of old imposed as a penance for the murder of a hermit in the reign of Henry II. Again Scott says that

> "Whitby's nuns exulting told,
> How to their house three barons bold
>   Must menial service do,
> While horns blow out a note of shame,
> And monks cry, ' Fie upon your name!
> In wrath for loss of sylvan game,
>   Saint Hilda's priest ye slew.'
> 'This on Ascension Day, each year,
> While labouring on our harbour-pier,
> Must Herbert, Bruce, and Percy hear.'"

N

THE rocky ledge runs far into the sea,
   And on its outer point, some miles away,
   A pillar of fire by night, of cloud by day,
The Lighthouse lifts its massive masonry.

Not one alone : from each projecting cape
   And perilous reef along the ocean's verge
Starts into life a dim, gigantic shape,
   Holding its lantern o'er the restless surge.

Like the great giant Christopher, it stands
   Upon the brink of the tempestuous wave,
Wading far out among the rocks and sands,
   The night-o'ertaken mariner to save.

      *   ❋   ❋   ❋

They come forth from the darkness, and
    their sails
   Gleam for a moment only in the blaze,
And eager faces, as the light unveils,
   Gaze at the tower, and vanish while they
    gaze.

"Sail on !" it says, "sail on, ye stately
    ships !
   And with your floating bridge the ocean
    span ;
Be mine to guard this light from all eclipse,
   Be yours to bring man nearer unto man !"

                            LONGFELLOW.

OUR LIGHTHOUSES.

" WE are safe! we are safe! there is help at hand ;
    Glad voices hail us from the strand.
  We are safe! we are safe! there is help at hand ;
    God bless the light of our native land !"

A PITCH BOX BEACON.

THERE can be no pleasanter object to the wanderer returning home to old England than the sight of the many lighthouses on our coast, and though I have already told you something about them, I am sure you will be glad to hear a little more. They tell of safety, home, and peace ; and whether perched on some wild headland looking down with kindly warning eye on the ocean, or standing on some dangerous rock, washed by the foaming billows, so lighting up the safe path—

"While the great ships sail outward and return,
  Bending and bowing o'er the billowy swells,
And ever joyful as they see it burn,
  They wave their silent welcomes and farewells."

In old times, in England, instead of these fine stone buildings, we had only stacks of wood set on high places; these were fired when enemies were seen approaching. Pitch boxes were next used; and in the reign of Charles I. we hear of lighthouses on the North and South Foreland ; but they were only timber buildings, on the top of which was placed a large lantern, and afterwards, when these were burnt down, as they all were, a flint tower was erected, on the top of which was an open iron grate, in which a large coal fire was kept burning all night, serving as a beacon in time of war.   You remember how, in the days of the Armada—

> " Swift to east, and swift to west, the warning radiance spread,
> High on Saint Michael's mount it shone—it shone on Beachy Head ;
> Far on the deep the Spaniard saw, along each southern shire,
> Cape beyond cape, in endless range, those twinkling points of fire."

It was also during the reign of Elizabeth that the French built the " Tour de Corduan," still the noblest lighthouse in the world.   It consists of a pile of masonry, forming galleries, surrounded by a conical tower, which terminates in a lantern.   Round it is a strong wall, which receives the shock of the waves.   There is in it a chapel, and some nice rooms for the keeper ; but now, as I want to keep to our own land, I will tell you the true and touching story about a lighthouse-keeper's daughter, and the brave deed she did.

Oh, what a terrible thing it must be to be on a ship tossing and heaving on a stormy sea ; men, women, and little children alike helpless before the angry winds and waves, that every moment threaten to engulf them in the dark waters ! How dreadful, even for those safe on shore, to see, far off, through the haze and the storm, a noble ship battling to the last, while indistinct figures of men and women are standing with outstretched arms imploring for help—for life —which brave, kind-hearted men dare not attempt to give them, for they know the cruel rocks that hide beneath the foam near that dangerous Northumbrian shore, and they themselves are sons, husbands, fathers, and may not risk such fearful peril.   "No, no, God help them, we cannot !" they murmur, as they turn away, wringing their brown hands for very pity, hardy men though they are. The money which the good steward of Bamborough Castle offers them, five bright golden sovereigns each, tempts them not as much as their own manly hearts do this bitter morning, when the *Forfarshire* steamer lies beating about the dreaded Farne Islands, where, in olden times, so many ships have struck.

Far out to sea, on some desolate rocks, stands the lonely Longstone Light-house, and with the earliest dawn, the keeper, his wife, and daughter watch the unfortunate ship strike on a cruel rock, and break into two pieces, one of which is at once carried off by the rapid current, which speedily washes away the shrieking passengers clinging in horror to each other.   Then, as the mist clears away, the pitying onlookers see that the fore part, on which are several persons clinging for dear life, still remains on the rock, likely at every moment to be washed off by the angry waves.

THE BEACON ON THE HILL.

"Can we not save them, father? Can we not do something for the poor creatures? Must they be lost, and we looking on?" cried the lighthouse-keeper's daughter, with the tears filling her soft blue eyes.

"Child, we cannot do anything but pray for them; see how the sea is raging, white with foam; it would be hopeless; we have but one little boat I am an old man, Grace; my arms are weak. It would be madness to attempt it! Grace, do not ask me; what would become of mother and yourself?"

"But I will go with you, father; I can row; I am not afraid of the storm and the wild sea; and we must not, cannot, let these people die on the Farne rocks before our very eyes. Oh, father! for God's sake, let us try! surely He will be with us in such a cause; let us trust to Him."

But her father shook his grey head, and her mother gently entreated her to be still. Poor woman! it was very hard—her husband, her child, wringing her hands and weeping for those helpless strangers perishing on the cruel rocks yonder. All day they watched, and still the wreck lay where it had struck; and still those nine far-off forlorn figures could be seen through the keeper's glass, frantically clinging to the broken timbers fast in the rocks. The storm at length abated somewhat, yet still the fierce sea raged, and the hardy fisher-men on the opposite coast dared not venture to attempt to save them, but looked on, and wondered, how long! Again the poor girl, brave and true of heart, cried and entreated: "Father, let you and I do what we can for these our brothers and sisters; but let us do our best." At last the old folks consented, and the pale, trembling mother herself helped to launch the little boat, and saw, with a beating heart, the two start on their errand of mercy. Hopeless, indeed, it seemed; but Grace was happy now. Over the waves, rowed by those willing hands, went that tiny boat; up and down it tossed in the foam. Little heeded Grace that her fair hair was floating in the wind, or that her garments were clinging to her all drenched with foam, that flew like a cloud; her thoughts were with that shattered wreck beyond, and the possibility of saving the poor wretches on it. Her father was inwardly praying that even if they should be able to carry back some of the survivors, they might not be all too exhausted to assist to manage the vessel. He knew that only at ebb-tide could the boat pass between the islands, that the tide would be flowing on their return, and that his own and this weak girl's arms would be quite unable, unassisted, to row the boat back to the lighthouse, in which case they all must perish. How desperate a venture it seemed now, after all, he

GRACE DARLING AND HER FATHER PUTTING OFF TO THE WRECK.

thought, as they silently moved over the waters, too anxious to exchange a word, or even a look.

But oh! what angels of mercy they must have seemed to that fainting band, as their boat at last came in view; what blessings from men and women must have risen over the roar of the waves, to encourage the noble-hearted pair, whose hearts rose as they at length, by God's blessing, reached the wreck, and rescued nine wan, worn fellow-creatures, the whole of the survivors of the ill-fated *Forfarshire!*

Need I tell you how Mrs. Darling, by her rocky home, watched that little speck on the ocean; how she prayed that they might return in safety; and how joyously, and proudly, and tearfully she welcomed them back to their poor sea-girt home? For two long days the storm continued, wind and waves raged without, but within the lighthouse thankfulness and gratitude were felt and shown to this noble family, who, at so great a risk, had saved nine precious lives, and now did their very best to share what little comforts they had, and to show kindness and hospitality to their starving, suffering visitors—certainly with no thought of reward or payment, for they had lost their all, but only out of a pure, unalloyed Christian charity, which it warms our hearts to think of.

But, for once, their kindly deed was not unnoticed. When the rescued people once more reached shore, and mixed with their friends and kindred, they told the story of their rescue—of the gentle, delicate girl, who, careless of peril and fatigue, had urged her father to come with her in storm and tempest to try and save them, and had done what the strong-hearted men of Bamborough had not dared to do, even for the promised gold. And the name of Grace Darling, the poor simple maid of Longstone Lighthouse, rang through England, and was spoken of in many a house; many a kindly message and rich gift were sent from far and near. A public subscription was arranged, and seven hundred pounds were collected, and presented to the wondering Grace, who could not be made to understand what she had done to merit the good fortune that now flowed in upon her. Offers of brighter homes and better positions could not tempt her to leave the lonely lighthouse on the rock, or her dear parents she loved and honoured.

But my true tale has, after all, a sad ending, I am sorry to say, for my brave, unselfish heroine had never been very strong. Too delicate a flower to flourish on those bleak rocks—money, and honour, and praise could not purchase health, or put colour into white cheeks, that blushed when the good deed was spoken of. Only four years from the stormy night, when she so bravely faced the storm, she died of consumption; and every eye filled with a regretful tear at the loss of the simple lighthouse maiden, Grace Darling, well deserving

the words written on the cross erected to her memory in St. Cuthbert's
Church near by :—

> " Pious and pure, modest, and yet so brave ;
>   Though young, so wise ; though weak, so resolute."

> " A maiden gentle, yet, at duty's call,
>   Firm and unflinching as the lighthouse reared
>   On the island rock—her lonely dwelling-place ;
>   Or like the invincible rock itself, that braves,
>   Age after age, the hostile elements,
>   As when it guarded holy Cuthbert's cell."

Grace was buried in the churchyard of Bamborough, near the old castle
school, in which she had years ago been clothed and educated ; and there you
may see the fair, silent figure of the maiden carved in stone, reclining on a
straw pallet, holding an oar, such as is used by the sailors on the Northumbrian
coast.

Bamborough Castle, in the shadow of which she lies, was once a strong and
mighty fortress ; a place of refuge or defiance for kings and nobles in the old
troubled feudal times. Now it is a house of kind deeds and charity, purchased
and bequeathed, as such, by Lord Crewe, Bishop of Durham. Its half-ruined
walls have been repaired, and now enclose schools for boys and girls ; while,
higher up, a constant watch is kept day and night, and should a storm arise,
signals flash to warn the poor bewildered mariner to avoid that most dangerous
mass of rocks, the Farne Islands. A lifeboat and other things necessary are
always kept in readiness; and should any poor creatures be wrecked, there are
beds and provisions at their service.

So, it has been well said, that on that perilous coast, Bamborough Castle
is to travellers by sea what the convent of St. Bernard, on the Alps, is to
travellers by land—a most blessed and welcome sight.

It is thought that the original fortress, of which one stately tower alone
remains, was erected as his castle and palace by Ida, King of the Angles, the
"Bearer of Flame," and that the sight of it so humiliated the oppressed and
vanquished Britons that they called it the "Shame of Berwick." Afterwards—

> " King Ida's castle, huge and square,
>   That from its rock looks grimly down,
>   And on the swelling ocean frowns."

was besieged by a pagan King of Mercia, who, wishing to destroy it, laid great quantities of wood under its walls. To this he set fire, but the wind rose, and blew the flames from the castle towards his own camp, so that he had to raise the siege and depart in a great hurry.

In old, old times there were lighthouses, the oldest of which was the Pharos, on the Egyptian coast, considered one of the seven wonders of the world. This was built some three hundred years before the birth of our Saviour. It is said to have been five hundred and fifty feet high, and to have consisted of several storeys, and galleries furnished with large mirrors (of polished metal, I suppose), in which shipping could be seen at a considerable distance. A fire was kept constantly burning on the summit, the light of which, historians tell us, could be seen forty-two miles from land.

And now for a pleasant little anecdote, showing what value has always been set on these " sentinels of the seas : "—

"About a hundred and seventy years ago we English folks were at war with France, as we often were in those days, and it happened that a French privateer, on the look-out for booty and prisoners, snapped up some of the men employed in building the famous Eddystone Lighthouse. The captors immediately returned to France, and brought their prisoners to King Louis XIV., expecting to be well rewarded for having stopped these

great English works; but the monarch ordered the workmen to be instantly released, and their captors to be put in prison, saying, right royally, ' Though I am at war with England, I am not so with all mankind, and this Eddystone Lighthouse will be of equal service to all nations.' Then he gave the Englishmen handsome presents, had them placed on a special ship, and sent them back to their work."

EIDER DUCK.

To those who take an interest in the birds that breed about our coast, a peep at these rocky islets will be a treat, for there they congregate in great numbers. Here is the Eider Duck—St. Cuthbert's Duck, as it is called. Poor things! it is their soft down, not themselves, that is wanted. They lay their eggs by the sea, in the grassy tufts popping up here and there, or in the many little hollows hidden away among the moss-covered stones thrown there by the raging of the North Sea. They make their nests of grass, moss, and dried sea-weeds, and then they line the little houses with the fine soft down from their own breasts; the poor patient things are often robbed of this twice in one season.

On some of the farthest out of these rocks, called the Pinnacles, there are crowds of Guillemots assembled, which present a very strange appearance, as they perch in straight, compact rows along the edges of the rocks, round which wash and splash the ever restless waves.

These odd-looking, brownish-white birds lay their eggs in places where you might

GUILLEMOT.

fancy they must be safe, but those who make a business of collecting eggs manage to get at most of them, even at the risk of their own necks.

BAMBOROUGH CASTLE.

THE RUINED CASTLE.

THE CASTLE.

As, in our "round and about" wanderings, we have so often come to the ivy-clad ruins of some ancient castle, and lingered to hear the tales and traditions associated with them, I think we may as well have a chat about the castles themselves, and about the kind of every-day lives that people led in them in the good old times, when they were, indeed, strongholds, before the days when shot and shell were used to batter down the defences of timber and stone. So strong were they, in many cases, that a comparatively few men, barred and bolted within, could defy whole armies without; and the monarchs of those troublesome times had often hard work to punish those turbulent nobles who, with their vassals and retainers, bade them defiance. You will see this at once if you examine this plan, which was more or less that on which most of the Norman fortresses were arranged. Such a stronghold, most likely, was that of the now ruined castle of Bungay, which once belonged to proud Sir Hugh Bigod—who, when offended by his king, exclaimed in a rage, as he mounted his steed and galloped away—

> "Were I in my strong castle of Bungay,
>   Upon the waters of Waveney,
>   I would not care for the King of Cockney,
>   Nor all his braverie."

However, as Sir Hugh was not even near his feudal shelter, he had to ride for his life with a whole troop of pursuers at his heels.

> "The Baily he rode, and the Baily he ran,
>   To catch the gallant Sir Hugh ;
>   But for every mile the Baily rode,
>   The earl he rode more than two,

Saying, 'Were I in my castle of Bungay,
Upon the river of Waveney,
I would not care for the King of Cockney.'"

He did at last get home; but then, the old ballad goes on to say—

" King Henry he marshalled his merry men all,
And through Suffolk they marched with speed ;
And they marched to Lord Bigod's castle-wall,
And knocked at his gate, I rede :
' Sir Hugh of the castle of Bungay,
Upon the river of Waveney,
Come, doff your cap to the King of Cockney.'

" Sir Hugh, of Bigod, so stout and brave,
When he heard the king thus say,
He trembled and shook like a May mawther,
And he wished himself away.
' Were I out of my castle of Bungay,
And beyond the river of Waveney :
I would not care for the King of Cockney.'

" Sir Hugh took three-score sacks of gold,
And flung them over the wall ;
Said he, ' Go your ways, in old mischief's name,
Yourself, and your merry men all ;
But leave me my castle of Bungay,
Upon the river Waveney,
And I'll pay shot to the King of Cockney.'"

So you see, after all. the rebellious subject did not get the advantage, as he expected.

But let us leave bold Sir Hugh, and examine the plan of a feudal castle, such as we may sometimes see in our rambles.

The outside of the walls usually consisted of the biggest stones near at hand, and the inside of fragments of stones, chalk, and mortar. The general shape and plan of a castle depended on the form of the ground occupied : the favourite situation was, for the sake of security, an eminence, or the bank of a river. The names and uses of the different parts remain to be described, for a better illustration of which I will show you a picture, which will enable you, with the help of a little explanation, to realise all the parts of one of those grim fortresses, about which we read so much and know so little.

The first outwork of a Norman castle was the *barbican*, a word supposed to be of Arabic origin. This was a watch-tower, for the purpose of noticing any approach from a distance, and was usually advanced beyond the ditch, at the edge of which it joined the *draw-bridge*. The next work was the *castle-ditch*, or moat, which was wet or dry according to the circumstances of the place, the former being preferred. When it was dry, there were sometimes underground passages, through which the cavalry could sally, and attack the enemy unexpectedly. Over this moat, by means of the draw-bridge, you passed to the *ballium*, or *baylcy*, a space immediately within the outer wall. This latter was called the wall of the ballium, and was generally flanked with towers, and had an embattled parapet. The entrance into the ballium was by a strong gate between two towers, secured by a *portcullis*, or falling door, armed with iron spikes like a harrow, which could be let fall at pleasure. Over the gate were rooms for the porter of

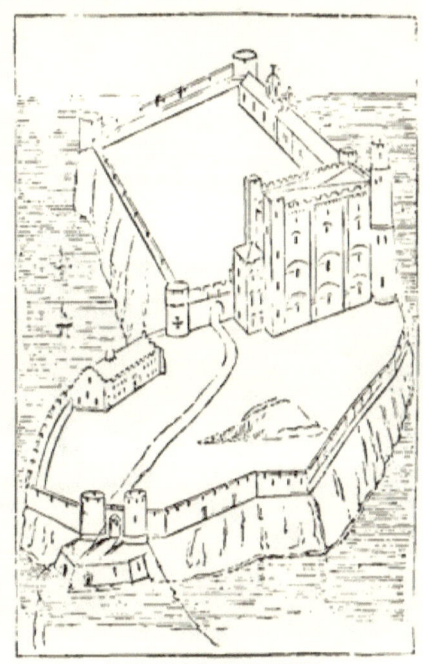

PLAN OF A NORMAN CASTLE.

the castle; the towers served for soldiers on guard. When there was a double line of walls, the spaces next each wall were called the *outer* and *inner* ballia. Within the ballium were the lodgings and barracks for the garrison and workmen, wells, chapels, and sometimes even a monastery; large mounts were often thrown up in this place to command the neighbouring country, for it was very desirable to see and not be seen.

On a height, and generally in the centre, stood the *keep*, or donjon, sometimes called *the tower*. This was the citadel or last retreat of the

garrison, and was often surrounded by a ditch with a draw-bridge, similar to those at the outworks, and with additional walls and towers. In large castles it was usually a high square tower, of four or five storeys, having turrets at each corner; in these turrets were the staircases, and frequently, as in Dover and Rochester Castles, a well. The walls of the keep were always of great thickness, which has enabled them to withstand the attacks of time and weather; the keep, or donjon, being the only part now surviving of many an ancient castle. Here were gloomy cells, appropriated as the governor's state rooms, the inmates, for the sake of additional strength, denying themselves the luxury of windows. Long narrow slits, or openings in the wall, served the double purpose of admitting a little light and enabling those within to discharge their arrows at the enemy below. But in process of time, and dating from the invention of gunpowder and the decay of the feudal system, castles

BARBICAN AND MOAT (CANTERBURY CASTLE).

became of little use as fortresses; the nation became more settled, and gradually the massive frowning towers of the time of William and Stephen were deserted for the pleasant baronial halls of a later date.

In the troubled times of Charles I., a commission was appointed to inquire into the state of these ancient castles, many of which were garrisoned and bravely held during the civil wars that followed afterwards. Not a few were destroyed by order of Parliament; others pulled down for the sake of the materials, or even to raise a more useful modern building on the pleasant site it occupied. But now, as we wander about our peaceful land, we find only ivy-covered remains, or are shown by some polite keeper round the delightful grounds.

Having shown you the castles, let me tell you something about the folks who dwelt in them, for I think most young people love to dream of the far-off times, when brick houses and plate-glass-windowed shops were not to be seen; but when, by sound of trumpet, knight and squire, page and retinue,

went gaily forth to throng about the tournament-ground where many a lance would be broken, and hard blow given and received, in honour of the blushing queen of beauty and her bevy of fair maidens—the chosen lady, who anxiously watched the combatants, and, the tourney over, rewarded the winner with a ring, or a rose, or a smile, maybe —the most valued prize of all.

PORTCULLIS.

In those early days, each proud baron's son had to win the dignity of knighthood for himself; and as it was no easy task, he began it as soon as he had passed seven years of age, when he was taken from all his women attendants, and was supposed to be no longer an infant.

The first step to future honours was to become a page, or varlet, that he might himself learn to serve and obey, and that he might one day the better command others.

The child was usually sent to form one of the household of some mighty baron—one of those warlike feudal chiefs who, surrounded by officers and squires, and keeping up a great state, would be the principal example and master in those very things the child could admire and early seek to imitate.

Poor little fellow! it must have been hard work at first, placed among strangers—men and boys—with no father to advise, no tender mother's voice to comfort him, no little gentle sister to play with him. He must, as soon as possible, learn the hard exercises of war. He must never complain

O

or cry at pain or hurt, on peril of being laughed at by the other young
nobles who were his mates in the same hard school where plenty was to
be done. They must serve their lord at the banquet, follow him in his
excursions, continually practise the management of arms and horses; as to
reading and such like, why that did not trouble them much—they left that
to the priest or clerk, whose business it was. A good knight's work would
be to fight, and to hold his own.

And so it went on, until our pretty page arrived at the discreet age of
fourteen; then, if he were considered advanced and bold enough, he exchanged
his dress and short plaything dagger, and flourished a real little sword, of
which, I dare say, he was very proud. Altogether, our page was usually very
happy, for, besides the rest, he had been taught music, singing, and dancing
—was strong and graceful, and by constantly being in the company of gentle
ladies and high-bred noblemen, doing for them every little service becoming
a modest youth, he generally acquired that pleasant grace of manner, that
"courtesie," which was the perfection of a true knight, such as we read about
in the old lays and romances most young people delight in.

But now, at fourteen years of age, a great event took place, for if he had
shown himself deserving, our little varlet was promoted from page to squire,
was allowed to set aside childish things, and take his first great step in the
path of chivalry. His new and untried sword was solemnly laid on the altar,
to be purified in the sight of God, only to be taken from it by a priest, who,
with many a prayer and benediction, hung it about the shoulders of the new
squire, who was now expected not only to give military service, but to hold his
lord's stirrups, carry his helm or shield, clean his armour, dress his horse,
serve him at table, and do other things, which to us seem menial, but to him
was all honourable employment.

When we read what was expected of these youths, we no longer marvel
at their being able, later on, to wear those ponderous suits of cold steel, and
to wield the great swords the men of to-day can hardly lift. These mere
lads had daily instruction in the wearing and management of arms and
armour; they practised springing on horseback or casting somersaults with
all their armour on, or sometimes they leaped on to the shoulders of the
horseman in front, only holding him by one hand. No wonder we hear
about after-deeds of strange valour and strength, when boys were trained in
this hardy fashion. Then, too, they saw the deeds of others, world-renowned,

for the squires followed their knights and lords to the battle-field, and watched, ready to assist with arms and hand, while the lord rushed to the encounter. The strict laws of chivalry forbade a squire to attack a knight; though, from some things I have read, I am afraid they did not always attend to this.

ARMOUR IN THE TOWER OF LONDON.

Now let us picture the eager young squire arrived at man's estate. He was twenty-one, and claimed the honour of knighthood from his master's hand, such occasions being held as great festivals—prayers, fasts, and confessions—and were generally fixed for some grand solemnity, such as Easter or Pentecost, or after a tournament. If the master, from some known ill-will, refused the honour, the squire could be knighted by another lord, who could bestow the "accolade"—generally three blows with a sword on the shoulder, with a few words, such as, " In the name of God and St. George, I dub thee knight ; be loyal, bold, and true."

When a King of England conferred the title of esquire upon any one not noble, he usually invested him at the same time with a silver chain and collar. The spurs of an esquire were of silver, those of a knight gold. Nor might an esquire enter the lists against a knight, nor strike him under forfeit of his right hand, nor wear ermine, sable, minever, nor any costly fur, which were reserved for knights alone ; and they must not take a special coat of arms.

But let us fancy our esquire invested with his new silver collar, safely through all his service, and about to enter the noble order of knighthood on the proud morrow. All this day of solemn preparation he was forbidden to laugh, talk, or take food of any kind ; then at meal-time he must sit silently at a table by himself, while his "godfather," as the noble who was to confer knighthood on him was called, and the fair ladies who were to arm him, dined gaily at another.

Then, at mid-day, he was led by his appointed esquires to the bath, where they washed his head with their own hands, and clothed him in the finest linen. In the evening he was conducted to the chapel, where he passed the night in silent watching and fasting. His sword, which was laid on the altar all night, was next morning publicly blessed by the priest, and hung round his neck, and he was led, with many ceremonies, into the presence of the knight who was to grace him with the honour of knighthood. He next knelt down before the lord or lady who was to invest him in his armour, and his attendants slowly clad him in his cuirass, cap, and hauberk, or coat of mail. Then his "godfather" placed his sword in his hand, and he was required to take three solemn oaths—"To speak the truth, to succour the helpless and oppressed, and never to turn back from an enemy." When the sword was fastened round his waist, and the spurs to his heel, he received a touch on the shoulder, and was bid to rise, "a knight, in the name of God, St. George, and St. Michael ;" and his noble "godfather," and the other knights present, gave him the kiss of peace and brotherhood, while all present pressed round to cheer and congratulate their new brother-in-arms.

This solemn ceremony was often followed by a great entertainment, at which, among much that was rare, the grandest dish was "a peacock in his pride," which a knight would carry in on a golden dish, and many a vow would be made over the bird, vows which would be held most sacred.

THE ACCOLADE: EDWARD THE THIRD KNIGHTING THE BLACK PRINCE.

And as this bird is often mentioned in the old records of English chivalry, I may as well tell you what was the method of dressing it and bringing it to table in our banqueting halls of the fourteenth century.

The peacock was carefully skinned; the head was wrapped in wet linen; the body stuffed with chestnuts, saffron, and gold powder; then it was slowly roasted; the skin, with its beautiful shining head of green and gold, replaced; and the large glittering tail spread out to its fullest extent, so that it was displayed to the greatest advantage on a costly golden dish, which the new-made knight received at the door from the hands of the greatest lady present, and bore, bare-headed, to the centre of the table, while trumpets sounded joyously.

From the end of the fourteenth century the glory and display of chivalry declined in England. Perhaps the long Wars of the Roses had aroused many habits and feelings opposed to knightly courtesy and generosity. Henry VIII. made many efforts to revive the old system of pomp and tournament; but even his own example was against the unselfishness and self-denial necessary for true chivalry. Knights became mere soldiers, and enthusiasm was disciplined, tamed, and paid for, so it soon died out.

Now, as we have said a great deal about the castles in which the people of long ago lived, let us have a peep at the manner in which these grand folk dressed themselves when they were not fighting and in cold steel. Among these old English fashions are some that strike us as very odd. Here is the description of an English dandy of long ago:—"He wore long-pointed shoes, fastened to his knees by gold or silver chains; hose of one colour on one leg, and of another colour on the other; very short breeches; a coat, one half white, and the other half black or blue; a long beard; a silk band buttoned under his chin, embroidered with grotesque figures of animals dancing."

Of course, it was not always fighting times in these ancient halls of old England, and one of the delights of nobles, before the days of fire-arms, was "hawking." Kings or courtiers, priests or fair ladies, seldom appeared in public without a falcon on their wrists; they even carried them to church, leaving them on the altar-steps during the service; and warriors, when attending public ceremonies, held the hilt of their swords in one hand, and their falcon on the other; but these noblemen only sent them up in pursuit of worthless birds, such as the heron, the crow, and the magpie; prey fit for food being worth money, was deemed only sport for an esquire or a common person.

In the famous Bayeux tapestry worked by Queen Matilda and her ladies, which is 227 feet long, and can still be seen in Bayeux Cathedral, King Harold is shown riding along with a hawk in his hand. These birds were trained and tended with the greatest care; and to prevent them from seeing and staring about, they wore a little cap strapped on their head—these, when the birds, some of which were very valuable, were the property of princes, were often decorated with feathers of the bird of Paradise. The hawks were carried to the chase in a cage, and while it rained, were held under a kind of flat umbrella. These birds were often trained by means of a bone, or imitation of a bird, on which was placed some meat; one man would hold the bone, and another person holding the hungry hawk, to which a string was attached, would take it to some distance, and uncovering its head, let it fly back to the food. Soon it would learn to fly off directly its eyes were uncovered at any heron or other bird, dropping down on it and killing it instantly.

HAWK IN THE TRAPPINGS.

So, you see, the gay ladies, and their war-like knights and squires and pretty pages, who dwelt in these ancient Norman castles, had their sports in time of peace, as well as their hard work in times of siege and war, and many a gay party would sally forth, hawk in hand, through woodland scenery, to discover the pool where lurked the stately heron, for in the days when hawking was such a fashion the "Heronries" were guarded and preserved with care. We so often hear of the heron that I should like to tell you what that bird is like, as a great many are still to be seen in the north of England. The common English heron is an awkward-shaped grey bird, with a large head set on a snaky neck; it has long legs set far back in the body, large feet, and a short tail—altogether, an odd, stately-looking creature. This solitary, melancholy-looking bird is still to be found in the neighbourhood of lakes and rivers,

PAGES COMPARING THEIR HAWKS.

where it stands in all kinds of weather for hours immovable, patiently watching for frogs or fishes, which it pierces with its strong sharp bill, and swallows whole. At night we may hear the sharp, unpleasant scream which announces that Sir Heron has given up the sport, and is flying off to the woods for shelter. If it is startled, it can fly up and up with a regular steady motion that soon carries it out of sight in the blue sky.

> " 'Tis the tall heron's awkward flight ;
> His crest of black, and neck of white,
> Far sunk his grey blue wings between,
> And giant legs of murky green."

The hawk's business was to rise up in the air above the heron, and then drop straight down and plunge its beak into the brain. Not a very pleasant sight, one might think, for fair ladies to enjoy ; too cruel a sight at best, it seems to me, who would rather see the heron standing dreamily on the stones, looking out for his supper. He, at any rate, only kills for the sake of satisfying his hunger.

MAGDALEN COLLEGE.

OXFORD.

"Like a rich gem, in circling gold enshrined,
  Where Isis' waters wind
    Along the sweetest shore
  That ever felt fair culture's hands,
      Or spring's embroidered mantle wore—
  Lo! where majestic Oxford stands."

THE grand old town, with its glory of pinnacles, towers, and spires, stands
in a plain in the midst of pleasant meadows thickly planted with trees; the

nineteen colleges which make it famous are mostly built in hollow squares, or quadrangles, as they are called. They are all handsome buildings, with chapels, halls, and libraries of their own; but the grandest and most famous is Christ Church, which was begun by Cardinal Wolsey. We can pass in through the Town Gate, where hangs the great bell that tolls 101 times every night, 101 being the number of foundation scholars it was intended for. Here is what some one wrote about its bells some years ago; it may interest you, as it did me :—

"It would not be right in our short account of the town to pass by without notice 'the bonny Christ Church bells,' which, ten in number, hang in the tower of the cathedral, and which were brought thither from Osney Abbey. Nor must we omit to mention 'the Mighty Tom,' the largest bell in England, which was also brought from Osney to this church. On hearing its well-known sound, the students of the university take it as a signal to retire within their respective colleges. The bell now called Great Tom of Christ Church had this inscription anciently on it :—

> In Thomæ laude,
> Resono BIM BOM sine fraude.

Which is bad Latin for—

> In praise of Thomas, I repeat
> My DONG! DING! DONG! without deceit.

Dr. Tresham, a Catholic priest, is said to have baptised this bell by the name of Mary, when it was removed from Osney to Christ Church, where he was canon, for the joy of Queen Mary's reign."

Now come into Christ Church Hall, with its carved oak roof—no other college has so large and fine a hall as this—and we can even peep into the huge, old-fashioned kitchen, where white-capped, white-aproned cooks are busy, at immense fires, roasting perhaps a hundred joints for the students' dinners. We cannot stop to describe so many buildings, or to tell of the good people who founded them in the olden times, that young men, both rich and poor, in days to come might be well taught by learned scholars—and I should have to write a very long list indeed if I told of all the clever and great men who have studied beneath the shadows of Oriel, Merton, or Brasenose. What an odd name that is, is it not, for a college? Some say it is derived from a "brasinium," or brewhouse, belonging to King Alfred, whose palace once stood here, and not from the big brazen nose, with a ring through it, which is shown over the entrance gateway. It was brought from a gateway at Stam-

MARTYRS' MEMORIAL.

ford, in Lincolnshire, to which place the students had retreated after a fight with the townsfolk of Oxford.

Here is Magdalen College, on the tower of which it is the good old custom to usher in the dawn of the first of May with music and a Latin hymn of praise.

Of course Oxford has its traditions, one of which relates to an ancient watch-tower, known as "Friar Bacon's Study," which stood on old Folly Bridge. Here it is said that the famous and learned Roger Bacon used to retire to study the stars; and as people in those days were very superstitious and ignorant, they accused him of practising magic, and treated him very badly in consequence.

For long afterwards all new-comers used to be warned not to walk near

THE ESCAPE OF THE EMPRESS MAUD.

the friar's tower, as there was a prophecy that when a man more learned than Roger passed under it, it would fall and crush him to death. I never heard of such a thing happening, though the old bridge has disappeared; but another is in its place, and standing on it we see across the pleasant Christ Church meadows, stretching along the banks of the sparkling rivers, the Isis and the Cherwell, where, if it is idle time, a few students are rowing up and down, preparing, may be, for the coming boat-race, the famous "Oxford and Cambridge," that by and-by will make such a stir all the country over.

WOLSEY'S PALACE OF HAMPTON.

Besides the colleges, halls, and churches, there are libraries, picture-galleries, observatories—not forgetting the Martyrs' Memorial, which stands near the spot where, in 1555, Archbishop Cranmer and Bishops Latimer and Ridley were publicly burnt, martyrs to the cause of the Protestant religion.

We must not forget the few ruins which are all that remain of a once fine Norman castle, about which I can tell you a story.

In the fighting days of King Stephen, when a great civil war raged in England, the Empress Maud was once closely besieged in that very fortress —so closely that it seemed as though she must surrender herself a prisoner. She tried a strange but brave venture for liberty.   It was bitter cold weather, and the country was all covered with snow ; so, waiting till all around was dark and still, the empress and a few friends, disguised in loose garments as white as the snow about them, stole out through the postern gate, and noise-lessly passed the weary sentinels, then through the camp of the triumphant besiegers—slipping through their very fingers, as it were—crossing the frozen Thames on foot, then away to Wallingford, where she met her brother with an army coming to the rescue—too late to save the castle, however, for it surrendered the next morning, a cage from which the bird had flown.

I have told you we owe the grand old Christ Church to Cardinal Wolsey. I daresay a good many of my little Londoners have been to Hampton Court Palace, and wandered about the great red-brick building, where kings and princes have wandered before them; at any rate, they have all heard of the grand domain, built and beautified by this great cardinal, "an honest poor man's son, of Ipswich." Here, in the days of his pride, he kept great state as a priest, holding high offices in the land, with a suite of above a thousand attendants and followers, who daily fed at his table. We can still see the huge fire-places, large enough to roast a fat ox whole, where the master cook attired in gay velvet or satin, with a gold chain round his neck, superintended his assistants and the children turn-spits. Some have told us that Wolsey was only a butcher's son—calling him a "butcher's cur;" and in a window of Oxford might be seen a dog gnawing the blade-bone of a shoulder of mutton—but as his great success and power must have made him many enemies, I do not know if this is quite true; at any rate, he was wonderfully clever, and a credit to his parents, whoever they were— for he was only fourteen years of age when he took his degree as Bachelor of Arts at Oxford. They called him "the boy Bachelor;" and the day came when, applying himself seriously to work, he was appointed chaplain to King Henry VIII., who, in a short time, made him Archbishop of York and Lord High Chancellor. He was the most powerful man in all England when he built this fine palace of Hampton—very much larger and more splendid than it is now. I need not tell you how he got into disgrace with his royal master, who would not be appeased, even by the surrender of this beautiful palace, that had been the pride and delight of its owner; who now at last friendless and deserted, went forth to face his enemies, crying, "Had I but served my God as diligently as I have served my king, He would not now have given me over in my grey hairs." And so the once gay "Boy Bachelor of Oxford," the mighty Lord Cardinal, the founder of Christ Church, the disgraced favourite, laid that forlorn grey head to rest among the monks of Leicester Abbey.

> "Speak thou, whose thoughts at humble peace repine—
> Shall Wolsey's wealth, with Wolsey's end, be thine?"

ETON COLLEGE.

WINDSOR CASTLE.

WINDSOR AND ETON.

IN the old, old days the Berkshire hills and woods abounded with all sorts of animals and birds. Wolves, wild cats, badgers, stags, foxes, and wild boars hid under the thick shadows of innumerable oaks and beeches, while the marshes near were crowded with snipe, geese, and swans. The people, who lived mostly in poor, wretched huts, were chiefly occupied with the care of wild swine and cattle. Berkshire pigs are celebrated to this day.

I suppose we ought to take just one peep at Reading, the county-town, where we shall see the remains of one of the grandest monasteries in the kingdom—the "mitred abbey of Reading"—where all poor persons or pilgrims found a comfortable shelter and food at their need. We can visit the spot, near Caversham Bridge, where a great trial by battle took place in the days of Henry II., when Robert de Montford accused Henry of Essex,

P

the king's standard-bearer, of having, during a skirmish in Wales, flung down the royal standard and fled like a coward before the foe, upon the mere rumour of the king's death. Henry and his warriors assembled in grand state to witness the hand-to-hand fight, which must end in death and disgrace to one of the two combatants, for in those days small mercy was shown in such a case ; to fall was to be considered guilty, whatever the charge.

Essex was defeated, and, as all thought, killed. The charitable monks of Reading offered to bury the traitor's body within their own holy bounds. Strangely enough, he soon recovered, and became a monk, living many long years within the old abbey walls—

> " The world forgetting, by the world forgot."

Three miles west of Oxford is an old manor house, which has a sad story attached to it—that of the cruel death of Anne Dudley, the fair wife of Lord Robert Dudley, Earl of Leicester, one of Queen Elizabeth's favourites—the very one she went to visit in such royal state at Kenilworth. Here the poor young lady had lived, sad and lonely, and many a busy country lass looked with pity on the countess in her solitary home. At last she disappeared—some say, was murdered. The place was long left uncared-for—it was thought to be haunted, and ballad writers tell us that—

> " The village maids, with fearful glance,
>   Avoid the ancient moss-grown wall ;
> Nor ever lead the merry dance
>   Among the groves of Cumnor Hall.
>
> " Full many a traveller has sighed,
>   And pensive wept the countess' fall,
> As wandering onward they 've espied
>   The haunted towers of Cumnor Hall."

We shall now travel southward and peep about Berkshire, for of all important places we must not forget to look at Windsor—the " Windle-shora," or winding shore, as it used to be called—with its proud Royal Castle and domain. From the battlements of yonder high Keep, or round tower, which used to be the prison of the castle, twelve fair counties may be seen ; and though it is twenty-two miles from London, " when ye weather is cleare, may easily be descryed Poll's steple." That 's what was said in the time of old St. Paul's ; you can prove its truth if you only mount

the winding stairs within the tower, though of course you will see the grand
dome of the cathedral instead of a steeple. Many kings and queens have

CUMNOR HALL.

lived and held their court here; and now our own royal family love to
retire from busy London to the quiet magnificence of the state apartments
of Windsor Castle.

The famous Edward III. was born here, and he loved fair Windsor so much that he had the old fortress, built by William the Conqueror, almost entirely taken down, and rebuilt the present stately castle, making it the seat of the most famous Order of the Garter, of which he was the much-honoured founder.

We get an idea of what the value of money was in those times when we read that the celebrated William de Wickham, afterwards Bishop of Winchester, was appointed to superintend the works for the payment of one shilling a day, while the sheriffs were ordered to send workmen, to be paid whatever the king might think proper. Some of these, being able to earn

better wages in London, ran away, but were caught and sent to Newgate prison, while the people who had employed them were dispossessed of all their property. Such was the liberty folks enjoyed in those days.

Almost all our English sovereigns have lived here; but it has changed very much from what it was in the rude Norman times, when strength was the great consideration in building. Queen Elizabeth raised a fine terrace, which was continued by Charles II. round three sides of the castle. George III. repaired the stately St. George's Chapel, and all the sovereigns since have added to and embellished it. Now it is considered one of the most splendid edifices in England.

Here it is that the installation of Knights of the Garter takes place. There are their seats and stalls, with the mantle, helmet, crest, and sword of each knight set on a carved canopy. Over the stall and over the canopy is placed the banner of each knight, and on the backs of the stalls are the titles of the knights, with their arms, finely blazoned on copper. When a knight dies, all these, excepting the plate of his titles, are removed to make room for those of a new companion, of whom there are twenty-five (always including the Prince of Wales), the sovereign forming the twenty-sixth; and the members are distinguished by wearing a dark-blue velvet band on the left leg, with a motto in golden letters. The same words are inscribed on the jewel of the order.

I wonder what was really the origin of this most famous Garter, with its simple motto, " Honi soit qui mal y pense." Some have told a pretty, pleasant

INTERIOR OF ST. GEORGE'S CHAPEL.

tale of the chivalrous Edward picking up a garter while dancing with the
Countess of Salisbury, and making it the badge of this new Order; but I am
afraid there is no foundation for this, the rather that Edward's head was full
of ideas of military glory. Determined to bind himself the boldest spirits
of the age, he invited brave knights from all parts to try their valour at great
jousts, to be held at Windsor every Whitsuntide, in honour of St. George; and,

in imitation of King Arthur's Round Table, he built the Round Tower, in which was placed a round table, made of fifty-two oaks, taken from the woods at

ETON COLLEGE QUADRANGLE.

Reading, so that all men who sat at it were equals—a kind of brave brotherhood, bound by a common tie, perhaps as typified by the circle of the garter —without beginning or end, and equal at all parts.

To these jousts came a noble company of earls, barons, knights, and squires, with crowds of ladies and fair damsels, to view the joustings and tourneys that took place at the great feast of St. George of England.

Later on Richard II. caused a joust to be cried at Windsor, and Froissart, the historian, tells us that forty knights and forty squires prepared to oppose all comers, "and they to be apparelled in green, with a white falcon; and the queen to be there, well accompanied with ladies and damsels." And so the joust was holden; but as the king and his nobles had quarrelled, not very many attended the summons, although "the queen was there in great nobleness," and was, no doubt, very disappointed.

See, yonder is one of the finest avenues in Europe. It is in a straight line of three miles long, leading from the principal entrance of the castle to the top of high Snow Hill, on which stands a huge statue of George III., and along each side stands a double row of stately elms—such a cool, shady walk on a summer's day. There is a tradition about an ancient tree that once flourished in the forest, called "Herne's Oak," that we shall hear as we stroll through the forest, because Shakespeare has made it famous, certainly not because it is true, for it is all about ghosts, and we know they never existed, whatever folk say.

Herne, one of the keepers of the forest, having committed some offence for which he feared to lose his situation, hung himself upon one of the branches of this oak, and he afterwards haunted that part of the forest, walking round about the oak at night, with great deer's-horns on his head, and frightening the country people.

The river Thames divides Windsor, which is in Berkshire, from Eton, which is in Buckinghamshire; but as a bridge joins the towns we will just step across and visit the fine old school, or college, of Eton, where—

> "Grateful science still adores
> Her Henry's holy shade."

The poet alludes to Henry IV., the royal founder, whose fine statue ornaments the principal square, or quadrangle, as you see in the picture opposite. He intended it for the educating of some seventy boys; now, I believe, there are over 700. These Eton boys have a fine library, and some precious manuscripts they prize highly.

ST. ALBANS.

*"Henry's mandate struck the fated shrine,
And sadly closed St. Albans' mitred line."*

Now we will take a fresh start, and I will tell you the story of an old, old town, only about twenty-two miles from London—of Verulam, as it was called when the Romans were masters in Britain.

"In Britain's isle was holy Alban born."

Alban, from whom the town is named, lived in the terrible days of the great Roman persecutions, when to be a Christian was to be a martyr. Alban was a Pagan, but a gentle-hearted man, and at great risk he gave a Christian fugitive shelter in his house, and after a short time was converted to the new faith, which Diocletian, the emperor, was determined to crush and destroy by fire and sword.

Soon there came a band of fierce armed soldiers, who all loudly demanded the surrender of Amphibalus, their prisoner. To save him Alban changed garments, and, while his friend was escaping, presented himself in his place. He was brought before the governor, suspected of having changed his faith, and ordered to sacrifice at the Pagan altar, and publicly worship Jupiter and Mars. This he refused to do, openly declaring himself a Christian. He was scourged and tortured; but he bore it all so patiently, that we are told even the executioner became a convert, and when ordered to behead the prisoner, cast down his sword, and declared that he too was a Christian, and ready to die for Alban, or with him. The two brave martyrs fell by the hand of a soldier, at a place called Holmhurst, near the city of Verulam, about the time of Constantine the Great. A church

HIGH STREET, ST. ALBANS.

was erected to Alban's memory, which was afterwards destroyed by Saxon invaders, but rebuilt by Offa, King of Mercia ; in consequence, says tradition, of a dream, in which an angel told him to seek for the body of Alban, the first British martyr, and place it in a proper shrine. The search took place, with prayer, fasting, and alms; and a ray of fire shining down on a particular spot, led them to seek there, and, sure enough, they discovered the wooden coffin where Germanus, the bishop, had placed it 344 years before. This coffin was taken to a little chapel without the walls of Verulam, and Offa is said to have placed a circlet of gold on the head of the martyr. He decorated the chapel with all the ornaments he could collect, and proceeded at once to erect a fine abbey, in which the remains of "Saint Alban" were placed. This abbey flourished for over seven centuries.

King Offa's abbey in due time passed away, and at the period of the Norman Conquest another one was built, of which there remains still the abbey-church and a large square gateway, a greater part of which is built of the same Roman bricks that were used in the city of Verulam. This church, in the form of a cross, is longer than any of our English cathedrals, and in it we can find traces of almost every style of architecture.

There have been two celebrated battles fought at St. Albans, between the rival houses of York and Lancaster, at the second of which fortune favoured Queen Margaret, and the Yorkists fled. The conquerors went at once to the abbey, where they were met by a long procession of joyful monks, who led them to the altar, that they might offer up their thanks at St. Alban's shrine; then the king, prince, and queen were entertained for several days at the abbey, which at that time was rich enough to afford them a royal welcome.

Eleven miles from here is Berkhampstead. Once it had a grand castle, defended in some parts by a triple moat; now there are only a few fragments of its massive walls left.

After the battle of Hastings, when William was coming by slow marches to take possession of his new kingdom, he was stopped at Berkhampstead by great trees and boughs, cut down and flung in his way by the Abbot of St. Albans. Being asked by the king why he dared to stop his army, the Churchman answered bravely, that "he had only done his duty; and that if all the Churchmen in the realm had done the same, they would have stopped an invader's progress."

"Then," said William, "I will soon cut their power down, beginning with you, proud abbot;" and he kept his word so well that by-and-by poor Abbot Frederic had to seek refuge at Ely, where he died; and William seized all the abbey lands between Barnet and London Stone, and would have ruined the monastery with a right good will had he not been persuaded otherwise.

Hatfield House is a place you will often find mentioned in your History book. Here it was that the Princess Elizabeth, having first been imprisoned in the Tower, was allowed to retire after Wyatt's rebellion. Here her stern sister, Queen Mary, visited her, and was well entertained with a grand

HATFIELD HOUSE.

bear-baiting, for in those days "gentle" ladies enjoyed such sports. It was while sitting under one of these ancient oaks that the princess first heard that she was no longer almost a prisoner but all a queen; and here she held her first privy council ere she left it to be crowned in London. We can still see the room in which she often sat and read, or sang, or played on the virginal or cittern, a kind of guitar. We hear, too, how in the great hall, now called the stabling, Sir Thomas Pope spent his money in amusing the captive princess with a rich masking, the pageants marvellously furnished, and at night a banquet of rich dishes. Upon the next day was played the "Story of Holofernes," which no doubt was very pleasant to see; but Queen

Mary hearing of it, soon let them all know she did not approve of such "follies and disguisings," as she plainly called them.

If you visit the present house (Lord Salisbury's), you will be shown many interesting things; among others, a large collection of arms that were captured from the Spanish Armada, the saddle-cloth used by Elizabeth when she made her famous visit to Tilbury, the oak cradle in which she was nursed, and the silk stockings presented to her by Sir Thomas Gresham.   No less than five valuable portraits of the maiden queen gaze at the visitor from perfect rainbows of ruff, pearls, jewels, and false hair, of which, I may mention, she had eighty sets; there are also portraits of many of her most celebrated subjects, in any amount of large trunk-hose, doublet, and ruff.

Ware, another place of interest, is to be found near.   You have, no doubt, heard of the great bed of Ware, an elaborately-carved bedstead of oak, twelve feet square, said to have been made by a journeyman carpenter for the use of the royal family of Edward IV.   It was to Ware that the celebrated John Gilpin's horse insisted upon going.   Do you remember the ballad ?

> "Said John, 'It is my wedding day,
> And all the world would stare
> If wife should dine at Edmonton,
> And I should dine at Ware.'"

Near the borders of Middlesex we come to the pretty Waltham Cross, which marks one of the places where the body of good Queen Eleanor rested on its way from Grantham, in Lincolnshire, to Westminster Abbey.   Her grieving husband, Edward III., placed a cross at each of the fifteen places where the sad procession stayed on its weary march.

The next place I mean to point out is the Rye House, where was formed a plan—called the Rye House plot—for the assassination of Charles II. and his brother.   It was arranged that as the royal party returned from Newmarket a cart should suddenly be upset in their way; during the sudden confusion, the king and the Duke of York were to be shot at from behind some bushes.   The plot failed; but the place is still standing—an ancient building over the gatehouse of a castle which has long since disappeared.

CHALFONT BURYING-GROUND, AND THE GRAVES OF THE PENN FAMILY.

BUCKINGHAMSHIRE.

WE can easily pass into the adjoining county of Buckinghamshire and peep in this quiet burial-ground, where lie the remains of the great coloniser, William Penn, his family, and friends. How solemn and still it is here! And how pleasant it is to sit and think of him who has been called the moral hero; he who conquered the fierce Red Indian by justice and wisdom at a time when massacres and cruel deeds had hitherto marked the steps of the white man through the forests of the Delaware. Think of him, simply distinguished by a blue sash, and all unarmed, surrounded by his band of English, Dutch, and other colonists, holding a treaty of peace, which was to buy the land fairly and honestly from the tribes assembled round him; the old men and the young, ranged rank above rank on the sward, their dark eyes fixed on the great *sachem* of the white men, whose motto was, " Peace be with you."

We might also visit Stoke Pogis (in its churchyard was buried Gray, the poet, who wrote that " Elegy in a Country Churchyard," which I hope you

STOKE POGIS CHURCH.

all know), where stood a quaint old manor house of the time of Elizabeth, which the same poet described as a building in which

> "The Huntingdon and Hattons there
> Employed the power of fairy hands
> To raise the buildings fretted heights;

MONUMENT TO THE POET GRAY, STOKE POGIS.

> Each panel in achievement glowing;
> Rich windows that exclude the light,
> And passages that lead to nothing.
> Full oft within the spacious walls,
> When he had fifty winters o'er him,
> My grave Lord-Keeper led the brawls—
> The seal and maces danced before him.
> His bushy beard and shoe-strings green,
> His high-crowned hat and satin doublet,

Moved the stout heart of England's queen,
Though Pope and Spaniard could not trouble it."

It is said that after William III. ascended the throne lately filled by a Stuart king, he visited Stoke, wishing to see over this ancient manor house ; but its then possessor, who had been a devoted adherent to his late majesty, James II., refused him permission, and stoutly declared that he "should never cross the doorway." "Tell him to go back," cried the old knight, wrathfully ; "he has already got possession of another man's house, and he shan't come into mine." His friends entreated, his wife fell on her knees—all of no use ; the king had to go his way—his curiosity was to remain unsatisfied, for he never saw the interior of the old house where Charles I. had been kept a prisoner, and where Queen Elizabeth had been royally entertained, with banqueting and many a quaint show, by Sir Edward Coke, the great lawyer.

In this neighbourhood are the famous Burnham Beeches, which, with their smooth stems and twisted roots, are a favourite study for artists.

High up among the chalky Chiltern Hills is one place I must not forget, and that is Great Hampden, the home of John Hampden, the patriot. In the old days of Edward the Confessor the Hampdens had settled here, and in later days it was proud and flourishing, until, if tradition speaks truly, one of the fiery race lost three valuable manors in a very foolish fashion—

"Tring, Wing, and Ivinghoe
Hampden did forgoe,
For striking of a blow,
And glad he did 'scape so."

And lucky, I think, too ; for the blow was given to the Black Prince during a quarrel which arose between himself and his host while exercising themselves in feats of chivalry, so common at that day.

Of course Queen Elizabeth visited Hampden, as is shown by an avenue called the Queen's Gap, which was cut through the woods for her convenience. There is a full-length portrait of her majesty still to be seen in the old room she occupied during this visit. But better you will love to peep in the long room, filled with books, and called John Hampden's library. He whose last words were, "O Lord, save my country!" lies buried in Great Hampden churchyard, near the house.

TRINITY COLLEGE, MASTERS' ENTRANCE.

CAMBRIDGE.

As we have lingered about Oxford, we must cross the country again to peep at Cambridge, the town on the Cam, our other great university. Queen Victoria went there in 1843, when her dear husband was installed Chancellor; and our clever Queen Bess, who seems indeed to have gone everywhere, visited it, and made a Latin speech to the scholars she found assembled there.

"DONS."

Wherever we go in this town we see handsome churches, and halls, and colleges, and we pass students in gowns and caps, and professors, better known as "Dons," who, we need not doubt, are very able teachers, especially of mathematics. Every year there is a great examination of the young men. Those who are successful are called "Wranglers," and the most successful of them all is the "Senior Wrangler" for the year, a proud distinction, I can tell you.

So many clever men have studied here, they would make up quite a list—Sir Isaac Newton and Lord Bacon, Pitt, Wilberforce, Bilney, Cranmer, Latimer, Ridley, Sir Philip Sidney, George Herbert, Fletcher and Waller.

Q

Byron and Macaulay the poets, and others.   In the garden is the mulberry
tree said to have been planted by Milton.

There are seventeen colleges and halls, the largest of which are Trinity
and St. John's ; but what you will like best to visit is King's College Chapel,
founded by Henry VI., with its marvellously-carved stone ceiling, ninety
feet high, which appears to be hung above us.   Milton, when a student
at Cambridge, wrote of this chapel :—

> "The high embowered roof,
> With antique pillars, massy proof,
> And storied windows richly dight,
> Casting a dim religious light."

The several foundations of both Oxford and Cambridge, now the two
great universities of England, were for the most part small and simple esta-
blishments at starting.   The numbers of scholars who rushed into these
schools from the first was something extraordinary ; nor were their character
and appearance less so.   They were described by Anthony à Wood as a
regular rabble, who were guilty of theft and all kinds of crimes and dis-
orders.   He declares that they lived under no discipline nor any masters,
but only thrust themselves into the schools at lectures, that they might pass
for scholars when they were called to account by the townsmen for any
mischief, so as to free themselves from the control of the magistrates.   Such
was the disorder of the two universities at one period, the violent quarrels,
not only betwixt the students and the townspeople, but also betwixt each
other, that many of the members of both universities retired to Northampton,
and, with the permission of Henry III., commenced a new university there ;
but the people of Oxford and Cambridge found means to obtain its dis-
solution from the king.   About thirty years afterwards they tried the same
experiment at Stamford, but were stopped in the same manner.

Jesus College has a chapel, in the form of a cross, with a large square
tower.   It is so pleasantly situated on the Cam that when King James
visited the town he said that if he lived in the university, he would pray
at King's, eat at Trinity, and study and sleep at Jesus.   I think if ever you
visit these places you will say, " What a good judge his majesty was !"

FLYING HOMEWARD.

IN THE FENS.

AND now, travelling northwards, we shall come to a county very different from those we have yet peeped at, for the surface of it is so flat that a part is lower than the level of the sea, so that strong embankments are raised to keep the water from breaking in and over this portion. There are no metals to be dug up here, but corn and grass flourish, and so do sheep and cows, and big dray horses. It is a famous place for cooks—so many things thrive for the larder in the way of ducks and geese, rabbits, hares, and water birds. In spite of the wet, it is a capital place for some things after all, though I should not care to live in the southern or "Hollow Land," which is part of the Fens, a plain surrounding the Wash, the name of which will remind you of King John. This Wash is an arm of the sea where, when the tide is out, a great deal of sand lies, along which carts can go. Do you remember how John, when retreating before Louis of France, took possession of Lincoln, and determined to cross the Wash from Lynn, in Norfolk? The army passed safely, but before the king could reach the other side the waves rose, washing away his baggage, and his crown and sceptre. John escaped, but died shortly after.

THE PASSAGE OF THE WASH.

We shall now visit old Lincoln, built on a hill above the Witham, crowned by its grand cathedral. Once it was a famous Roman town, and we can still see a gateway and wall erected by those long-ago conquerors. Norman William built a brave castle, which stood many an attack, until the Civil Wars of Charles I., when the Royalists, having retreated to the cathedral and the castle, the fortress was stormed, and the inmates soon forced to surrender.

LINCOLN CATHEDRAL.

" Never will the marble arch grow duller
   For the tread of feet beneath its span ;
Never the rich window lose its colour
   For the wondering eyes of gazing man "

There is little of the castle left now, except a gateway, some windows, and a ruined staircase, by which we can ascend to the top of the ruins and take a survey of the cathedral. It has almost the highest tower in England.

Following the Witham through the flat fenny country you see Boston at the mouth of the river. Once this Boston was, next to London, the greatest seaport in England; but the Witham became partly choked up, and so lost its consequence.

Stamford is another celebrated town, which once had a strong castle, and was fortified with walls and towers. For a long time there was a curious and barbarous custom in this place. Every six weeks before Christmas the butchers of the town provided the wildest bull they could buy, and having placed it for the night in a stable belonging to the alderman, sent round a bellman in the morning to warn every one to shut their shops and doors; then the bull was turned out in the streets and a chase commenced. Men, women, and children, flourishing clubs, ran helter-skelter in pursuit of the enraged creature, never leaving him till he dropped down exhausted, when—

> " A ragged troop of boys and girls
> Do pellow him with stones."

I am glad to say this horrid butcher's custom has long ceased.

Sixteen miles from Stamford is Croyland Abbey, once one of the grandest monasteries in England. I will show you a picture of it, that you may see how its glory has departed. Yet what a fine ruin it is to look upon!

Another place worth noting is the quaint old triangular bridge. It was built exactly where the Wyse and the Welland joined, its centre being over the middle of the waters. By its step is carved a rough quaint figure of some Saxon monarch, supposed to be Ethelbald, King of Mercia, holding a great stone in his hands representing a loaf, it is thought. This Ethelbald, about a thousand years ago, founded a monastery in Derbyshire, and to this retirement came many, among others a youth weary of warfare and the world. He became a monk, and was afterwards styled St. Guthlac. Wishing to show a good example, he lived a close ascetic life, and at length determined to put entire trust in Providence. He left the monastery, rambled on, he knew not, cared not, where, and at last seeing a small deserted boat on a river, determined that wherever it chanced to land him there would he abide. He was wafted to Croyland Isle, which, like Ely, is no longer an isle, and here built a hut, and lived and died so famed for piety that the king determined to found on the spot a monastery to his memory.

But now, though I have so much more to show and to say, I must stop for

CROWLAND ABBEY.

want of space, not for want of interesting subjects ; and I know no better part-ing words than—Study your country's history, not only from school books, but from the records left in its grey stones, its language, and its traditions, and learn by every means in your power to be a credit to Old England.

LOOK from the ancient mountains down,
  My noble English boy;
Thy country's fields around thee gleam
  In sunlight and in joy.

Ages have rolled since foeman's march
  Passed o'er that old, firm sod;
For well the land hath fealty held
  To freedom and to God.

Gaze proudly on, my English boy,
  And let thy kindling mind
Drink in the spirit of high thought
  From every chainless wind.

There, in the shadow of old Time,
  The halls beneath thee lie
Which poured forth to the fields of yore
  Our England's chivalry.

How bravely and how solemnly
  They stand, midst oak and yew!
Whence Cressy's yeomen haply framed
  The bow, in battle true.

And round their walls the good swords hang,
  Whose faith knew no alloy,
And shields of knighthood, pure from stain—
  Gaze on, my English boy.

PRINTED BY CASSELL & COMPANY, LIMITED, LA BELLE SAUVAGE, LONDON, E.C.
70,973

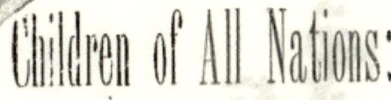